INVASIVE S P E C I E S

Contents

INVASIVE SPECIES

JAKE REBER

jake   reber

1 ZERO DRIFT ONE

SILVER LANDS ARE OOZING DRIFTING OUT THE
IMPOSSIBLE BREAK WITH ROGUE DNA CODES OF
ZEROES UNDER A VAST SILENT FREQUENCY --

LANDS ARE THE EMBERS OF SPACE LASHED BY

TOXIC MAS^S DEATH IN AMBIENT RECESSION
INTO CIRCUITS OF GOVERNMENTAL AUTHORITY
IN *REVERSE* BURNING DRIFTING THROUGH THEIR
TANGIBLE EXISTENCE INDEBITED TO SHOPLIFT
FROM THE CONSUMER BACKED UP ATROPHYING

PARADES OF CHILDREN RIOTING WITHOUT
TRACES

NO DOOR IS STREAKED WITH IT WITH ROGUE
DNA CODES OF *ANAMORPHATIC SYMBIOSIS* WITH
MULTITUDES OF COMMAND SYSTEMS INTO A
VOID WHICH WIRES ITSELF TO T E R R O R TO
BE TURNED AGAINST AUTHORITY THE HYDRA HEAD OF

ATROCITY PROJECTED ON WORLD   BEGIN DEEP SPACE VAPOURIZED IN DISCARDED STOCKPILES OF *TERMINATION* CONVERGING UPON LIQUID NITROGEN WITH THE INTERIOR ALREADY INSIDE FENCES OF ENTROPY INVOLUTION

SPACE VAPOURIZED IN PARALYSIS OF HUMAN POTENTIALS SPREAD OUT INTO LEG MUSCLES WHICH *SEDUCE* YOUR CONTRACTS SLICE ACROSS THE **ABYSS** IN   V E R T I G O   OF RECUPERATION AND ENDS WHERE BARELY ACTIVE GLANDS STILL CARRY OUT INTO LEG MUSCLE WHICH CO^{N}SUM^{E}S THE **E M B E R S** OF ESCAPE AND ARE JOINED *ARRANGEMENTS* OF MEAT DISINTEGRATING IN CARDBOARD CITIES OF RUBBISH LOCKED NO COUNTER MEASURE IS EFFECTIVE AGAINST HOLLOW BLAZES CRACKLING IN A DEADLY FUNGUS (THE VIRULENCE OF ANNIHILATION) ALL YOUR PARANOID EYE IN DISCARDED STOCKPILES NEAR CHILDREN OF BLAZES CRACKLING IN TEN MILLION PARAGRAPHS OF ASSASSINS ATROCITY PROJECTED ON WORLD BANKS OF ANARCHO TECH DRAWN AND PARASITES

THE CRACKLING IN GENERATIVE SEQUENCES OF DESIGNER CAPITALISM AND UNBINDING ALL THESE ARE BURNING DRIFTING OUT NO COUNTER HEGEMONIC STRIKES THE VIRTUAL

NIGHT PANORAMA OF SPACE **ALGORITHMIC DATA BLEEDING** BACK *INSIDE FENCES* OF HALLUCINATORY HELICOPTER GUNSHIPS DELIVERING TRANSNATIONAL

SEEDBEDS OF **INVASIVE PLANTS**

PANORAMA OF PULSION AND MOUNTAINS FROM INCREDIBLE JOURNEYS THROUGH MICROSCOPIC INJURIES AND BECOME THE GLOBAL SIGHTSEERS TOUR THE RUINS NEWSREELS OF

MUTANT CITY **THE HYDRA HEAD OF** COLLAPSE HUMAN POTENTIALS **SPREAD OUT INTO THE** HELPLESS **HEAD OF   E S C A P E BURNING DRIFTING OUT**

CITY INTERZONE THE ENVIRONMENT SLOWLY REVEALING THE WORLD BLEEDS OF **ADDICTIVE** *SUBVERSION OF TISSUE* FOR MELANOMA AND SUCKING UPON THE

LAST

SHAKING oS^{C}ILLA^{T}ING AT THE ICE WITH THE CLINICAL ***HYPERMARKETS*** LONG RANGE ~~BULIMIC OVERDOSE NONE OF~~ **~~ANAMORPHATIC SYMBIOSIS~~** ~~WITH ROGUE DNA CODES~~

OS^CILLA^TING AT PLACES WHERE BARELY ACTIVE
GLANDS STILL CARRY OUT INTO DEEP SPACE
LASHED BY ITS OWN **STICKY BLACK**
VEINAL LIES AND

CONVULSIVE FREQUENCY OF **TRANSCENDENCE** COLLAPSING
INTO SHAKY MUSCLES WHICH BLEED IN
AMBIENT RECESSION INTO TECTONIC TREMORS
OF SOLAR RADIATION MORTIFIED
EXCREMENTAL

FREQUENCY AND BREAKING UP ATROPHYING
PARADES OF STRAYS V A G A B O N D S AND
MOUNTAINS FROM THE OPENING OF
ANNIHILATION ALL YOUR CONTRACTS SLICE
ACROSS

BREAKING UP INTO *TECTONIC T R E M O R S* OF
REPULSION FAMINE QUOTED ON THEMSELVES
TO THE **IMMUNODEFICIENT**
MEMBRANES A RUST SPECKLED WITH
MULTITUDES OF LESIONS FIERY CONES OF
GOLDEN VAPOUR RUNS **ENERVATED** RESCUE
ROUTINES HURLING KILLER PROGRAMS INTO
BARBARIAN PLATEAUS OF
TECHNOGENETIC

INFORMATION

TECTONIC TREMORS OF *HALLUCIN A T O R Y* VISIONS DELIVERING FLUIDITY IN TRANSNATIONAL ~~PAYLOADS OF HALLUCINATORY ORDER~~ AND TREMORS OF CRIMINAL INFECTION ONLY WHEN THE **SUBVERSION AND ENTROPIC** CIRCUIT BOARDS IN **NANO TECHNOLOGY** AND *PANIC AND PANIC* THE UNDERTOW OF

HELICOPTER GUNSHIPS DELIVERING TRANSNATIONAL PAYLOADS OF WORMS

COLLAPSE HUMAN IDENTITY SPLICING THE PULSING RHYTHM OF THEIR FUNCTIONS ORGANS OPEN FLOWERING INTO LESIONS FIERY CONES OF HOLLOW BLAZES CRACKLING

HUMAN LINEBREAKS UNDER THE SIDEWALK WITH IT WITH CLANDESTINE MALEVOLENCE AND ACCUMULATORS OF CAPTURE HEATSEEKERS IMPLODING EVERYTHING IS STREAKED WITH LESIONS AND MACHINE COMBINATIONS NOT YET REALIZED PASS THROUGH ~~SEVERAL~~ GRADUALLY DEGRADING STATES **INDEXED** TO ENTER OR GO OUT NO DOOR IS ALREADY **COMBINATIONS** NOT YET REALIZED PASS THROUGH **DESERT** AND REDESIGNED AS ALL CLOSED CIRCUITS OF HOLLOW BLAZES CRACKLING IN A VAST SILENT REALIZED PASS THROUGH THE CONTROL SHIVERING IN THE INFORMATION WAR FREE THE APEXES OF THE NORTH ENCHANTING LOCAL POPULATIONS AND

PASS THROUGH THE ICE WITH THE
HEAD OF DESIGNER
CAPITALISM AND THEIR
THEOPOLITICAL MALCONTENTS PEDDLING THE
CONSUMPTION IMPOVERISHED MILITARY WINGS
THROUGH EXCLUSIVE CLOSED NETWORKS OF
REVERSE RUSTLE OF

FEVERISH

HALLUCINOGENIC DEGREES OF
COMMANDMENTS ALL BURNING DRIFTING OUT
THEIR VIRULENT THEOPOETICS

2 ALIEN INVASION SOFTWARE

VENOM-SOAKED MEMBRANES AND
DEEP D I G I T A L TECHNICS **PERFORM**
ILLEGAL SURGERY ON THEMS E L V E S
SHOWER ^{O}F COL L A P S E D HUMAN
POTENTIALS SPREAD OUT IN REPTILIAN
CAMOUFLAGE VANISH$_{IN}$G

POPULATION OF *COLLAPSE HUMAN* *AND DARK*
VANISHING *WITHOUT* **FORENSIC TRACES**
IN G E N E R A T I V E SEQUENCES OF SHIT TO
METRIC SCALES OF GOVERNMENTAL **AUTHORITY**

MEMBRANES A TRICK OF
BLACK CAPITAL CONSUMES
THE URBAN RESTING
SATELLITES OF EATING
CLONED BECOMINGS
EJACULATING STREAMS OF
ADDICTIVE SUBVERSION

STRANGE WILDLY
MUTATING
ANTHROPOIDS
GATHERS ON
WORLD
EXCHANGES AS
THE ARMPITS THEN
AT CONVULSIVE
FREQUENCY AND
CALCIFICATION
WELCOME TO MAKE THE

WILDLY MUTATING
ANTHROPOIDS ~~GATHER ON~~ **WORLD**
~~BANKS OF SEX~~ *AND* *PARASITES* ~~THE FRAUGHT~~
~~PATHWAYS AND THEIR FUNCTIONS ORGANS OPEN~~
~~LIKE SNAKES~~

~~MUTATING ANTHROPOIDS GATHERS ON A HIT OF~~
~~REVERSE TRANSCRIPTS IN OPAQUE POOLS~~
~~IDENTIFYING AND FRAGMENTING THE CITY~~
~~INTERZONE INFECTED BY~~ ~~VORTICULAR MASS~~

~~ANTHROPOIDS GATHER ON THE PLATEAUS~~
~~SECRETING TOXIC VAPOURS OF SEMI~~
~~AUTONOMY BEFORE DEMISE PLAGUES OF SPACE~~
~~VAPOURIZED IN WHITE HEAT ENGENDERING~~
~~CRISIS~~

CHANNELED ON A VAST SILENT FREQUENCY
SPACE LASHED BY
VORTICULAR MASS CRASH FREEZING OF EATING

**BORDER OF LAVA
APPEARING FIRST
AROUND THE COLD AND
PARASITES** THEN **FREEDOM
NARCOTICS SOLD IN AN
ELECTRONIC VISION
REALITY CRASH**

STATES PREVIOUS
ARRANGEMENT OF
INSANE SPECULATION
(SHEDDING OF FORM)
TO THE DROPPER AND
ITS NIGHTMARE
ENEMY THROUGH
THE ADDICT SEIZES

SPACE LASHED BY AN ALIEN INVASION OF
HOLLOW BLAZES CRACKLING IN GENERATIVE
SEQUENCES OF ASSASSINS OF STRAY
VAGABONDS AND DRIFTING SPECIES LASHED BY
WESTERN LANDS ARE LIQUIDATED IN COUNTER
MEASURES IS REJECTED BY DEEP
SUBTERRANEAN *LANDS ARE JOINED*

ARRANGEMENTS OF BACTERIA

SPREADING OVER STREAMS OF NOMADIC
ENCAMPMENTS FORTIFICATION OF STATE
POWERLESSLY AGAINST THE LIDS OF
**INTERPRETATION RIDE OUT NO MEMBRANE
IMPERMEABLE EVERYTHING IS DROWNED**

AND PLUNGES IN *AMBIENT RECESSION*

INTO THE COMPOSITE CITY SHAKING
OSCILLATING AT CONVULSIVE FREQUENCY

OF *TRANSHUMANS SQUATTING IN REPTILIAN
CAMOUFLAGE*

TRACER FIRE SPEWING FROM DESPERATE
MIGRATIONS FROM PROLIFERATING ORGANS

VOMIT OF TISSUE FOR MELANOMA

AND FINDING IT LOCKS ONTO ITS BLACK FIRE
SPEWING FROM PROLIFERATING ORGANS OF
RULING ASSEMBLIES RUNNING BLADES DRAWN
AND ARTERIAL BLOOD COLD EXPLOSION OF ALL

THESE ARE SPEWING FROM THE FINAL
UNIFICATION OF SPACE ON THE NEED TO ALL
THESE ARRANGEMENTS OF INSANE
SPECULATION *S H E D D I N G*
THEIR PROLIFERATING
ORGANS VOMIT OF ENTRY INTO DEEP
SPACE ON A HIT OF ANDROID ANDROGYNY WHICH
HANGS OPEN FLOWERING INTO TECTONIC *CONTROL*
HELIOCENTRIC PILES OF CRIMINAL INFECTION
AND **SYNTHETIC GERM KILLERS** HYSTERIA
SCHIZOPHRENIA AND ILLICIT COMMERCE A
NEXUS OF RULING ASSEMBLIES
RUNNING TOWERS POLICING THE
INTERIOR ALREADY AMONG YOU DOWN TAKING
WORLD BANKS OF THIS COMES FROM WITHIN
TRACKING ITS BLACK MARKET

PRAISING THE ANTI
OEDIPUS CHRIST
YOU SHALL KNOW THIS INFECTION AND
SO **PARAMILITARY FORMATIONS** OF
REALITY CRASH FREEZING OF TRIANGLES
AND LINES DOWN IN CATASTROPHES OF
CORPOREAL MATTER LINING IN THE ANUS
WHICH HANGS OPEN FLOWERING INTO AN
ALIEN INVASION SOFTWARE FROM INCREDIBLE

JOURNEYS THROUGH IMMUNODEFICIENT
MEMBRANES A FRENZIED BINGE OF SADO
MASOCHISTIC GRATIFICATION NOTHING BUT
SUN PRECIOUS STONE TABLETS OF DESPERATE
MIGRATIONS IN INFORMATION AND BROKERS OF
ANARCHO TECH HACKED AND FUTILE REACTION
UNICELLULAR BLOWING APART OF DEAD LINES

FROM DESPERATE TRANSFERS FROM THE

BLOODY SUNRISE *WHICH*

BLEED IN A FRENZIED BINGE OF HALLUCINATORY

DISORDER AND BIOTECH

CORPORATIONS DELIVERING THE CELLS LIKE

WATER IN DISCARDED LIQUID POOLS OF
MONETARY EXCHANGE AS ALL MENTAL

BREAKDOWN REDESIGNED BY *VORTICULAR*

MASS CRASH THE INCREDIBLE
JOURNEYS THROUGH DESERT AND SUCKING
UPON SNOW WITH SCRAPS AND THEIR
FUNCTIONS ORGANS OPEN FLOWERING INTO
MUNDANE PLATEAUS OF JOURNEYS THROUGH
IMMUNODEFICIENT EXCLUSIVE CLOSED
NETWORKS WHICH HANGS OPEN FLOWERING
INTO LESIONS FIERY CONES OF REPULSION
FLAMES QUOTED ON WORLD EXCHANGES
THROUGH SEVERAL GRADUALLY

DEGRADING STATES INDEXED

TO ALL CLOSED NETWORKS WHICH CONSUME

THE CITY INTERZONE AND FINDING IT AS THE
DIGESTIVE

DESERT CHOKES THE INSERTION OF
INTERZONE WHICH PROLIFERATES AND GROWS
WITH CHAOTIC MALEVOLENCE MUTATING CELLULAR
STRUCTURES ON THE LIDS OF SPACE
VAPOURIZED IN JUNGLES AND STRIPPED TO
MATTER LINING THE SUBVERSION OF
NUCLEAR BLASTS OF PLASTIC RUBBISH
SECRETING *TOXIC VAPOURS* THROUGH THE *SEMI-
AUTONOMY OF MOUNTAINS* FROM STASIS AND
SPRINT HEADLONG TOWARDS THE UNDERTOW
REVERSE RUSTLE OF ESCAPE IMPERSONALLY
ACHIEVED THE MOVEMENT OF WORMS FROM
INCREDIBLE JOURNEYS THROUGH DESERT AND
UNBINDING ALL CLOSED NETWORKS WHICH BEWARE
THE MADNESS OF SUICIDE A THREE INCH STASIS AND
MEANING IN THE FOLDS OF

TRANSCENDENCE COLLAPSING

INTO FRAGMENTED PLATEAUS OF GOLDEN
VAPOUR RUINS ENERVATED RESCUE ROUTINES
HURLING *KILLER PROGRAMS AND*
DEATH RATTLES OF SUNSTROKES AND

ILLICIT COMMERCE A RUST SPECKLED WITH
ROGUE DNA CODES OF STATE CRAWLS WITH
IMPACTS UPON

RIFT VALLEYS EXCAVATED AND STRUNG ON
THEMSELVES SHOWERS OF BLISTERS RISING

LIKE LITTLE AIR BUBBLES UNDER THE DROPPER
AND PANIC AND

VALLEYS EXCAVATED BY THE REVERSE
BLEEDING BACK INSIDE FILLING THE LIVER
AND SYNTHETIC GERM KILLERS HYSTERIA
SCHIZOPHRENIA AND **B E C O M E T H E S A N D S**

VORTICULAR MASS EXCAVATED BY AN OFF
CRASH THE SIGNAL VIRAL CONTROL
COMPOSITE CITY THE SHIVERING IN GENERATIVE
POINT WHERE ONE SEQUENCES OF BACTERIA
WRONG TERM IN SPREADING OVER IMMENSE
WHIRL OF BLISTERS DUNES OF RATIONAL
RISING LIKE SNAKES THOUGHT SCATTERED

EXCHANGE OF MASS
CRASH THE HYDRA HEAD OF NULLIFICATION AT
THE FINAL UNIFICATION OF PANIC AND RIOTING
FOR MELANOMA AND THEIR SKIN CLOSING

***CRASH THE MELTDOWN OF MACHINIC
ALLIANCE FLOWING GRACEFULLY* ACROSS THE
FORTIFIED ENCAMPMENTS OF ENTROPY
INVOLUTION THROUGH THE** PULSING
RHYTHM OF FREEZING URBAN SPRAWL IN
DISCARDED JUNKPILES OF CONSUMPTION
IMPOVERISHED WIRELESS WINGS OF DESIGNER
CAPITALISM AND RIOTING FOR THE DROPPER
AND ALL URBAN SPRAWL IN AMBIENT
RECESSION INTO AN INFERNO OF
SOFTWARE CRASHES ALL MENTAL
BREAKDOWN REDESIGNED AS CONSUMPTION TO
BE FREE FROM SPRAWL IN AMBIENT RECESSION
INTO FLESH FORMS WHICH CONSUME THE

NETWORKED AMBIVALENCE OF SOFTWARE CRASHES ALL MENTAL BREAKDOWN REDESIGNED

invasive species

3 VAST SILENT FREQUENCY

ALL **GOLD** STANDARDS *MELT DOWN*
IN PARALYSIS OF LARVA APPEARING FIRST
AROUND THE FLASH OF THEIR THEOPOLITICAL
MALCONTENTS SCANNING

INFINITY THE BLOODY SUNRISE WHICH
HANGS OPEN *FLOWERING* INTO WOUNDS AND

CATASTROPHES OF **ANDROID ANDROGYNY**
WHICH CONSUMES THE PLANNED ECONOMY
COMMUNISM

COMPOSITE CITY SHAKING *OSCILLATING AT* ONCE
COLD AND GRATIFYING SURRENDER
NOMADOLOGIES OF CRIMINAL INFECTION
ONLY WHEN THE NORTH ENCHANTING LOCAL
POPULATIONS CITY INTERZONE **KILLS** THE

ENVIRONMENT SLOWLY
REVEALING THE VOID CONCEALED BENEATH ITS
BLACK CAPITAL CONSUMES THE BOREDOM OF SUICIDE

WHILE GLOBAL SIGHTSEERS AND ZONES
INFECTED BY ESCALATING THE RED NIGHT
PANORAMA OF XENOCIDAL STATE SCIENCE

FLYBLOWN *CORPSES OF*

OVERLAID BRIDGES

JUXTAPOSED PATHWAYS GROW WITH AN
INFERNO OF ELECTRONIC BURNOUT AND PANIC
IN CLINICAL HYPERMARKETS   LONG
RANGE ANOREXIC RECESSION   GO OUT NO
MORE THAN A SLOW

SPIRALIZED WEALTH SYSTEM OF ADDICTIVE
SUBVERSION AND COMMANDMENTS THAT END
THE RULING ASSEMBLIES

VIRULENCE OF   DEADLY FUNGUS
HAZMAT SETTLEMENT   THE SIDEWALK
IN THE RED NIGHT   WITH MULTITUDES
PANORAMA OF TISSUE   OF DEMISE
FOR MELANOMA AND   PLAGUES OF
BREAKING UP   STRANGE
ATROPHYING   ATTRACTORS FUSING
PARADES OF SLUDGE   SEQUENCES OF
AND SLIME   DIGESTIVE TRACK IN THE
                            INTERZONE INFECTED

BY FUNGUS THE GAPS BENEATH OR UNDER THE
NORTH ENCHANTING LOCAL POPULATIONS WITH

PROSTHESES **CIRCUIT BREAKER** OF
SUICIDE A *NEXUS* OF ENTRY INTO THE PLACE OF
OVERLAID BRIDGES JUNCTIONS PATHWAYS AND
BROKERS OF TERMINATION CONVERGING UPON
THE INDIGESTIBLE IS FREE TO ENTER OR GO OUT

DEAD HUMANITY POWER AND JUNGLES AND RIOTING FOR MELANOMA AND BLADES

REFLECTING *SHOCK WAVES* OF ENTRY INTO LESIONS WHICH BLEED IN ROADS WHERE *UNDEAD ARMIES OF ANAMORPHATIC SYMBIOSIS* WITH ROGUE DNA CODES TOXINS IN DISCARDED STOCKPILES

HUMAN IDENTITY UNDER THE ZONE ARE THE NOMADS UNDERGROUND SHEDDING OF ANNIHILATION ALL GOLD STANDARDS MELT DOWN WITH ROGUE DNA CODES

OF DESIGNER CAPITALISM AND RIOTING FOR WHERE BARELY ACTIVE GLANDS STILL CARRY OUT IN PARALYSIS OF FORM TO INDETERMINACY AND STRIPPED TO PIECES LUXURIOUS NAKED LUNCH OFFERED

POTENTIALS SPREAD OUT INTO BARBARIAN PLATEAUS OF MELTING THE SCIENTIFIC APPARATUS OF TELEONOMIC COMMUNICATION FALLING TO THE BORDERLINE AND

SPREAD OUT THE PLAGUE WILD ALLIANCES OF ENTROPY INVOLUTION THROUGH MICROSCOPIC INJURIES AND THEIR *TANGIBLE EXISTENCE IN WHIRL OF LAVA APPEARING*

VAST SILENT FREQUENCY OF COLLAPSE HUMAN POTENTIALS

SPREAD OUT INTO TECTONIC TREMORS OF THE NEED TO ENTER OR SHORT RANGE ANOREXIC SILENT FREQUENCY OF PANIC THE SUBLIMINAL

HUM OF HOLLOW BLAZES CRACKLING IN
BLEEDING BACK INSIDE FILLING THE
IMMUNODEFICIENT MEMBRANES A HIT MARKET
A SYRINGE WIRED TO BE TURNED AGAINST THE
CLINICAL HYPERMARKETS LONG TERM
ANOREXIC RECESSION OR SHORT RANGE
BULIMIC OVERDOSE ON BUILDINGS IN
OPAQUE POOLS IDENTITY UNDER A
PLAGUE WILD ALLIANCES OF HEATED

PHOTOSYNTHESIS

BIOMECHANICS CUT UP THE HYDRA
HEAD OF CAPTURE ZONE ARE *IMMANENT TO
MATTER LINING THE FLESH* AND ALCOHOL
SICKNESS IN **WHITE HEAT** ENGENDERING CRISIS
AND DEATH RATTLE OF CAPTURE JOINED
ARRANGEMENTS OF HOLLOW BLAZES
CRACKLING IN A CATHECTED MOTOR OF
ADDICTIVE SUBVERSION OR TERMINATION

CONVERGING UPON *DEADZONES*

AND TRACER FIRE SPEWING

ARRANGEMENTS OF XENOCIDAL STATES WHERE
ONE WRONG TERM IN GASTROELECTRIC

CONVULUSIONS OOZE FLUID WHICH

FALLS DEAD DRIPPING OF **ANAMORPHATIC
SYMBIOSIS** WITH WOOD BRICK CONCRETE
GLASS PACKING CRATES CORRUGATED IRON
WHERE ALL YOUR CONTRACTS SLICE ACROSS
THE FLESH AND UNBIND ALL STRUCTURES

jake reber

4 ART &
ITS CORPSE

DEEP SIMULATIONS WE CAN NO LONGER
REMAIN MERELY SKEPTICAL WITHOUT
BECOMING **PARADOXICAL** IN POSITION AND
THE DEATH OF THAT HEROISM DID SAY THERE WILL BE
TRANSAESTHETICS A PROCESS OF BYZANTIUM
THE MASTERY OF RECUPERATION ENDS AS
CONSUMPTION OF SEXUALITY CRITIQUE AND
AESTHETICS IN ADVERTISING AND
POWERLESS

TOWARDS THE FANTASY OF AUTO COLLISION
CRYOGENIC FREEZING URBAN RESTING SATELLITES
OF CYBERNETIC
CONTROL

**VANISHING POINT OF
CYBERNETIC CONTROL
TOWERS POLICING THE
INESCAPABLE PATHS OF
DEAD HEADS OF
SUNSTROKES AND
EQUIVALENCE TO
ANNIHILATE TO
DISAPPEAR**

HELIOCENTRIC PILES
OF A DUAL
CONJECTURE AND

POINT WE LIVE WITH
CAUSES GONE ALL
HUMAN POTENTIALS
SPREAD OUT THERE
BEING STRAINED TO
DECONSTRUCT ITS

SALVATION IN **VERTIGO** A RELATIONSHIP
WITH CLANDESTINE MALEVOLENT GOVERNMENTS
OR SYSTEMS OF GOVERNMENTS BANKING CARTELS

IMPRISONING THE **O R I G I N A L**

ART AND ITS CORPSE EVEN ITS PURITANICAL
AND ILLICIT COMMERCE A NOSTALGIC
BOURGEOIS **REFRAIN THE SANDS** OF SHIT
TO BETTER INGEST INCOMING

AESTHETICS HAS SO ON CATASTROPHIC
WASTAGE VIRUS MUTATIONS YET REALIZED AND
MACHINE COMBINATIONS *NOT* EXCEL THROUGH
IMMUNODEFICIENT MEMBRANES A MAN WHO

**ALWAYS THOUGHT
SIDING WITH IT MUST
INSIST ON MORE VALUE
SACRED THE UTOPIA OF
EQUIVALENCY ARE
ONLY AN OFF SIGNAL
VIRAL**

REMAINED
CLANDESTINE
MALEVOLENCE O
GOVERNMENTS O
SYSTEMS OF
**TRANSHUMANS
SQUAT IN
COMMODITY** IF I
MEAN THOSE WHO

CLAIMED TO ITS PARTIAL

CLANDESTINE *INTERMITTENT AMBIVALENT*
PROBABLY BECAUSE ALL EFFECTS ARE
ALREADY LIBERATED WHAT IS COMPLETE JUST
THE TEMPTATION TO WALTER BENJAMIN S FACE

INTERMITTENT AMBIVALENT PROBABLY BECAUSE
WE ARE LIQUITED IN A SYRINGE WIRED TO
CONTINUE ON MORE OBJECT THE TOP TEN
MILLION PARAGRAPHS

AMBIVALENT PROBABLY BECAUSE THEN AN
AESTHETIC **REPRINTING** OF CULTURE ART
EVERYDAY IN WATER IN COUNTER HEGEMONIC
STRIKES THE SOLUTION THE VIRAL PROBABLY

BECAUSE ALL EFFECTS HIT OF IMAGES I SAY
WHAT IS WHY THEY HAVE SAID I CALL IT

SENTIMENTAL EXPRESSION AGAIN BECAUSE HE
SPOKE OF EVERY DOMAIN THE EXTERIOR WHICH
STARTS WITH VALUE WHICH HAS DISAP PEARED
JUST AS FOR ALL THESE ICONOCLAST I MEANT

ANYTHING WAS AN AURA OF NUCLEAR
ARSENALS OF ASSASSINS OF SHOCK WAVES OF
ANAMORPHATIC SYMBIOSIS WITH PROSTHESES
AND FROM IT WOULD

THE FRAGMENTS COME
FROM INCREDIBLE
JOURNEYS THROUGH
DESERT AND SUCCESS A
CENTURY ITS VALUE
AND UNBINDING ALL
CLOSED CIRCUITS OF
ANTI OEDIPUS CHRIST

DO YOU WANT TO
DISAPPEAR WARHOL
MADE SACRED AS
OFTEN IS DIFFICULT
TO SPEAK WHEN THE
WORLD SOMETHING
MORALIST
METAPHYSICAL
TRADITION A
PROFUSION OF DISAPPEARANCE AT PLACES

WHERE BARELY **ACTIVE** GLANDS STILL
BEING REHABILITATED TODAY HAS BECOME
ICONOCLASTIC IN THE METAPHYSICAL
TRADITION **A SKIN OF HALLUCINATORY ODER**
HELICOPTER GUNSHIPS DELIVERING
TRANSNATIONAL PAYLOADS OF COURSE ALL
WE ONLY CARRYING BLACK VEINAL AND

TRADITION; A STORY FULL OF

CYBERNETIC

CONTROL

SHIVERING ^{IN}

CULTURAL

AESTHETIC

TERMS INTO BARBARIAN PLATEAUS OF
DIGESTIVE TRACK OF ANARCHY LIQUID
POLITICAL OR ELICITING ANY MEANS OF

EXQUISITE DREAM

WHICH NOT FAR ^{FROM} THIS
TRANSCENDENCE C O L L A P S I N G INTO
MUSEOGRAPHIC REPRODUCTION **OPAQUE**
T E M P O R A L I T I E S IN HUMAN
DISASTER ZONES OOZE ACROSS THE UNEVEN
STRATA

AND ELECTRIC CRYSTALS BLEED^{IDEOLOGICAL}
TRADITION A SENTIMENTAL
AESTHETICIZATION ^{WETWARE} STATED THAT
ART IS DEALT WITH ABSOLUTE COMMODITY WITH
ITS **SALVATION** ^{IN} **ITSELF** MORE NEGATIVE

AN ANTI TRADITIONAL CHALLENGE OF SUICIDE
ATTEMPT AS FOR *SPECIES* THAT PAINTED HIS
DISASTER POLITICALLY DESPERATE MIGRATIONS
FROM IT DENIED

THAT TO LEAVE **NO MEMBRANE
IMPERMEABLE** EVERYTHING HAS NOTHING
TO METRIC SCALES OF REPRESENTATION ALL
MENTAL BREAKDOWN **REDESIGNED AS** EACH
**IMAGE GODALWAYS RESOLVED BY
EXCEEDING ITS POWER** *OF SKIN CLOSING DOWN*
**WITH PROSTHESES CIRCUIT BREAKER OF
STRANGE WILDLY MUTATING
ANTHROPOIDS GATHERS FLOWS** LIBERATED
**THE PUBLICIZING GENIUS THAT IMPLICATED
BOTH THE COMMODITY ON THE** AUTOMATIC

MACHINE **LIKE A WEAK SOLUTION DIALECTICS
IS**

WARY OF *CAPITALISM* AND THE
AESTHETIC TURN THAT SURROUND US
AND NOW WE HAVE THE DISTINCTION BETWEEN
A WORLD AND ALL ALIENATING DISEASEs

CULTURE UNDERSTOOD AS THREAT AND
EXPRESSES ITS PROBLEMS THAT ILLUSTRATED A
TRUTH OF ACCOMPLISHING THEM A *FATAL*
INDIFFERENCE TO USEFULNESS AND

GENERAL A E S T H E T I CI Z A T I O N OF
XENOCIDAL STATE POWERLESSLY AGAINST THE
SHELVES OF ACCOMPLISHMENT SINCE
OBSESSED WITH NO DIALECTIC BETWEEN THESE
ARE CIRCUITS

THAT CONSTITUTED THE DEAD BATTERY
MUSEUM ^{IN} ONLY SIMULATION ORGY AND ALL
RULES OF GOVERNMENT WEAPONS ART THERE
JOINED ARRANGEMENTS

ALWAYS THE
CONTRARY IT SPAWNS
A KIND OF THINKING
WE LIVE WITH
MULTITUDES OF
UNKNOWN INSECT
COLONIES GORGED ON

MODERN SOLUTIONS
TO SURVIVE WITH
CAUSES GONE ALL WE
CAN ONLY BLEED
PERSPECTIVES
DIFFICULT

WARY OF CANCER THEN
IT WAS NO DOOR IS CARRIED OUT ^{IN} OTHERS
FATALLY CONSUMED BY SIMULATION WHEN I
WAS

DISTINCTION BETWEEN THESE ARE PREPARING
FOR SIM ULACRUM THAT WALKS AMONG YOU
COLLECTIVELY FACED WITH EARLIER
MORNING SIGHTS OF SEDUCTION **B E T W E E N**
NATURE AND DISAPPEARANCE A THOROUGHLY

REALIZED REALITY CRASH DISASTER
CONSUMPTION IMPOVERISHED MILITARY WINGS
OF AUTO SUGGESTIVE WEALTH NATURE AND
THIS DEEP ANALYSIS UNDER THE

TECHNOLOGICAL

ATHLETICISM AND TRACER FIRE

SPEWING FROM DEAD IN CROSSTOWN LIBIDINAL
FLOWS OF SYSTEMS AND CULTURE WILL BE
TURNED AGAINST AUTHORITY AND ANTI

OEDIPUS CHRIST PRAYERS AND PROCEDURES
DOWN ^{IN} REALITY WHERE WE DO NOT DESTROY

REALITY DISAPPEAR WARHOL MADE SACRED
AGAIN IT BY TENTS BIVOUACS FABRICS AND
BLEEDING *BACK INSIDE FILLING THE FARTHEST*
THE OTHER MORE SOMETHING TOO CONSCIOUSLY
TOO BANALLY OBVIOUS I MAY HAVE BEEN ONE IF

THIS CHOICE BY ITS SIGHT CULTURE A

DEADLY BANALITY I AM NOT

ENLIGHTENING OR ENLIGHTENED NO MOMENT ^{IN}
CANCEROUS GROWTHS OF GOLDEN VAPOUR RUNS
ENERVATED RESCUE ROUTINES HURLING ^KILL_ER
PROGRAMS OBVIOUS I KNOW BUT ON A SENSELESS
REPETITION OF SACRIFICE ^{IN WETWARE} INVENTED
THE HEMORRHAGE OF SEXUALITY CRITIQUE AND
NEUROTIC *MATERIALIZATION*
ALWAYS A SIMULACRUM TO RAISE PROBLEMS IN
ART AS MARX WROTE AND VIRTUALLY IT STILL

LIVES PARADOXICALLY AS THE BODY NO

ANNIHILATION

FOR THE SELF

ALREADY DOES

NOT EXIST THOUGHT

SCATTERED DEBRIS IN THIS CURRENT LIQUID STATE OF FLOWS AND INDIFFERENT QUALITIES THIS HOLLLOW FOR SIMULATION IF WE CAN SPLICE INTO SCRAPS AND SUBMACHINE GUNS DRAWN AND VIRTUALLY EQUIVALENT THEY HAD DISAPPEARED THEREIN LIES THEIR SECRET OF SACRIFICE WITH ART AND SHOULD NOT CONSIST IN DISCARDED STOCKPILES OF TERMINATION CONVERGING UPON THE EXPLORATION OF FEVERISH *HALLUCINOGENIC* DEGREES OF EVERYTHING INTO DIRECT LINE LINKS WETWARE WANTING TO DESCRIBE AND GROW INDIFFERENT QUALITIES AVOIDING ALIENATION ART AND THE FETISH OBJECTS AND MODERN EASY SOLUTION FACED WITH DISEASE BEING ANY MEANS FOR SPECIES THAT IS AFTER THE SIDEWALK WITH ALL PROBLEMS THAT HAVE THE ONLY SOLUTION FACED WITH OFF SIGNAL VIRAL CODES OF TRANSCENDENCE COLLAPSING IN ITS NIGHTMARE ENEMY THROUGH IMMUNODEFICIENT EXCLUSIVE CLOSED CIRCUITS **SAME GOES FOR POETRY** WHEN STRIPPED TO CIRCULATION OF

DRIFT BLACK

BOXES ^{IN} ITS **NIGHTMARE** ENEMY THROUGH IMMUNODEFICIENT MEMBRANES A MOCKERY OR ANTIHERO OF SEXUALITY ^{IN} **DISSIPATING** STRUCTURES ONLY AN ULTRA COMMODITY INDIFFERENCE THIS FOREIGNNESS IS ORIGINAL ANYWAY

5 TIME CRYSTALS

POETRY AND *CORROSIVE* *JUICES*
FOLDING THE BANALITY ^{IN} IT MEANS GIVING
THIS COMMODITY ^{FROM} *WETWARE* INVENTED
THE DERISORY AND ADVENTUROUS

PAINTING NO LIVING ZONES IS
BEAUTY AUTHENTICITY AND
MEANING THE **CARDIOVASCULAR**
NETWORKS WHICH THE VERTIGO A
NEWLY VICTORIOUS FETISH AND
NEXT

SHOULD PASS THROUGH IMMUNODEFICIENT
MEMBRANES A STORY FULL OF
TRIUMPHANT REAPPEARANCE TODAY HAS
THOROUGHLY *ENTERED* REALITY SOME
JUSTIFICATION FOR ANOTHER UNPREDICTABLE
DEATH

SHOULD TAKE AWAY ^{FROM} A NEXUS OF
LIBERATION OF SPLICED ^{WETWARE} WE ARE NOT
BELIEVING ^{IN} OTHERS STREAKED WITH
MULTITUDES

PASSING THROUGH LOSS OR VIRTUALLY
EQUIVALENT THEY OVERWHELM THE
PROPHECY THEREFORE CIRCULATING ALL
HUMAN POTENTIALS SPREAD OUT THERE WILL

BE THROUGH A MUTANT CITY
SHAKING oscillating AT THEIR
SECRET OF A ROUTINE OF TELEONOMIC
COMMUNICATION FAILING TO RAISE PROBLEMS
HAVE NO ENCHANTED SIDE ENIGMATIC AS IT IS
BY *DENYING* THE ECSTASY OF AUTO
SUGGESTIVE WEALTH COLLAPSING
GOVERNMENTS IN *PHARMA* CARTELS
IMPRISONING *SIDEEFFECTS* OF EVERYTHING
WHERE NOTHING WAS ACCOMPLISHED UTOPIA
NEVER ACCOMPLISHED ^{IN} VERTIGO A
SKEPTICAL CRITICAL PARADOXICAL
WHEREEVER BARELY **ACTIVE** GLANDS
FORMED IN DESIGNER CAPITALISM AND PAINTING NO
DIALECTIC BETWEEN A HIDEOUS DRY HUNGER
THE PULSING RHYTHM OF TRIUMPHANT
SIMULATION BUT AN APPEARANCE UNTIL ALL
MODERN PASSION KNOWN AS CONSUMPTION TRIES
REVIVING IT AND SHOULD FEAR THE ENCHANTED
SIDE OF *GOLDEN VAPOUR* RUNNING UNTIL ALL
AESTHETIC REPRINTING OF COMMODITIES THAT

HAVE THOROUGHLY ENTERED REALITY IT STILL WAS RESOLVED
AND IRONIC QUALITIES THAT THESE PROBLEMS ART BORN

ALL MADE SUBMACHINE DROOL TO BECOME
MONSTROUSLY *UNFAMILIAR* BUT THE
ASCETICISM OF SADO MASOCHISTIC
GRATIFICATION SUN EXPLODES INTO NOTHING
BUT WHEN IT HAS RESOLVED BY
DEFINITION AESTHETIC JUDGMENTS ARE
ALREADY TAKEN PLACE IN REACTORS OWN
DISAPPEARANCE OF THE BUREAUCRATIC AND
MELTING THE ASCETICISM OF ASSUMPTIONS
ALL *MENTAL DEICIDE*
REDESIGNED AS PEOPLE ONCE EVEN
GREATER SPEEDS BUT SUN SODOMIZING
THE PLANNED ECONOMY COMMUNISM
FASCISM FUNDAMENTALISM FREE PROBLEMS
HAVE EXPLORED ALL VISION BREAKDOWN
REDESIGNED AS THREAT I MEAN THOSE WHO
WHISPER INTO THE TECHNOLOGICAL

PRECISELY IN THIS TRANSCENDENCE COLLAPSING
IN CRITICAL DENIAL BECAUSE THEY OVERWHELM
THE DICE HAVING EXPLORED ALL MENTAL
BREAKDOWN REACHED A SUCCESSFUL SUICIDE
STREAKED WITH SCRAPS AND BREAKING UP INTO
CIRCUITS FLOWERING INTO BANALITY SOMETHING
DIFFERENT TURN WETWARE

ATHLETICISM AND ALL MACHINES HAVE POWER
AND ARTERIAL BLOOD COLD AND TRACER FIRE

SPEWING ^{FROM} STASIS AND CULTURE *WAITING FOR SPEAKING* AS COMMODITY ALREADY LIBERATED THE PROBLEM OF VALUE BY OBSESSING WITH DEATH WHEN WARHOL ADVOCATED THE FIX OF SEX AND UNBINDING ALL YOUR RESOLVED AND UNBINDING ALL OF SHIT TO *DISAPPEAR WARHEADS* PAINTED CRASHES OR FIGURATION GO INTO ^{SOFTWARE} OPPOSES THEM EVEN SELF DESTRUCTION OF MARVELOUS COMMUTABILITY BECAUSE IT LASTED FOR THE MODERN ERA GIVING THIS ONE LAST TRY OUT OR ^{IN} BUT ONE COULD ONLY SOLUTION TO TRY REVIVING IT THE OTHER IS DIFFICULT TO ALL MODERN SALIVA THE MASTERY OF SHOCK STRANGENESS OF CULTURE

DEMISE PLAGUES OF CIRCULATION NETWORKS WHICH IS ORIGINAL IT *SENTIMENTAL* **EXPRESSION** AFTER TWENTY YEARS AGO THAT HEROISM DID NOT PROBLEMS HAVE ALREADY TAKEN PLACE OF PRODUCTION PROGRESS REVOLUTION ARE **ACCELERATING**

^{IN} THE G R E A T *TRANSCENDENCE* OF *ANNIHILATION* ALL MENTAL BREAKDOWNS **REDESIGNED** THAT HAD DISAPPEARED ^{FROM} DESPERATE CONCLUSION ^{INTO} COMMODITY A MEDIA TODAY AND I SAY WHAT WE CALL IT AS EACH DAY REALLY POSED IDEALLY DEFINED ART ITS PROBLEMS THAT ARE

ALREADY MANUFACTURED BE TRULY
MODERN CHALLENGE OF CIRCULATION
NETWORKS OF ILLUSION THE TOXINS DEFINED
AS ART MATERIALIZED EVERYWHERE ART NO
COUNTER MEASURE IS NOT CONSIST ^{IN} TERMS
PREDETERMINED AN ULTRA COMMODITY A
SICKNESS OF ART EVERYDAY ^{IN} COMMODITIES
WHICH NOT BECAUSE WE ALL BREATHE
THESE TWO SYNTHESIS IN OUR ENERGY ^{FROM}
SOMEWHERE ELSE ART ASSUMES ALL THESE
ARE REALLY IDEALLY DEFINED ART IN
SALVATION ^{AND} MANY ARTISTS ENGAGED ^{IN}
WETWARE TO SOLUTION THE PRESENCE OF
MUSEOGRAPHIC SIGNS AND SUCKING UPON THE

CIRCULATION OF HUMANITY

AND CALCIFICATION WELCOME TO THE
TRULY MODERN WORLD PROBLEMS HAVE
LEFT WITH ABSOLUTE THERE IS AFTER THE
INFORMATION WAR FREE TO BOTH
CONTEMPORARY AND GENETIC ONES THAT
REVIVES AND SURROUND US WE LIVE ^{IN}
COMMODITIES MORE O B J E C T ITS SALVATION
IN FACT *SIMULATED GODS VISION* TO STAND OUT NO
EVEN ITS MEANING THE RECUPERATIVE
INTESTINE IS FREE ^{FROM} IT AN ELECTRONIC
MIASMA OF RATIONAL THOUGHT SCATTERED

DEBRIS ^{IN} ONLY CARRYING RAISED BUT ^{IN} REPTILIAN CAMOUFLAGE **VANISHING WITHOUT** ANY MEANS GIVING THIS VANISHING POINT WHERE WOULD BE A FALSE SIMULATION THIS ART WANTS MY RELATIONSHIP WITH THE **D E**

A T H AND FANTASTICAL BESIDES ENIGMATIC AS EACH DAY WE INHABIT A NOTE OF COURSE ALL SPLIT PROBLEMS THAT HEROISM DID SAY PROSTHESIS INSTEAD OF OUR *CULTURE* ART TO THIS SURPASSED ^{IN} WHICH WOULD DO WE CAN PROBLEMS ART THE APPEARANCES OF ***TRANSPARENCY AND SYNTHETIC GERM KILLERS*** HYSTERIA SCHIZOPHRENIA AND FETISHIZED *ABSTRACTION* ^{IN} TEN MILLION PARAGRAPHS OF SEDUCTION PROFOUNDLY *SEDUCTIVE* MORE THAN MARKET ^{IN} MAKING ART I SAID THAT ACCORDING TO REPRESENT GOD FOR *POETRY AND DELINEATE* SINCE EVERYTHING SEDUCTIVE TIED TO PERFECTION WHICH CONSUMES THE RITUAL WE

ONLY CARRYING OUT THE FACT

SIMULATED GOD ^{IN} REALITY IT AS A ALTHOUGH I MUST VANISH OF COMMAND SYSTEMS OF HIS SOUL BOXES ^{IN} PARALYSIS OF FEVERISH HALLUCINOGENIC DEGREES OF RATIONAL THOUGHT SIDING HAVE COMPLETELY UNFOLDED EVEN ITS OWN CORPSE AS IF THEY HAVE EXPLORED ALL KNOW HOW TO ALL SENTIMENTALITY ^{IN} **OPAQUE POOLS** SPOKEN THROUGH IT MUST TAKE YOU

PREFERENCES WE FIND OURSELVES ^{IN} BUT
PERHAPS ONE COULD AT ITS FUNCTIONALITY
THEN ECHO ENTHUSIASTICALLY ABOUT IT
CANNOT BE A PROFUSION OF EVERYTHING

I FIND SOME JUSTIFICATION FOR SEVERAL
GRADUALLY DEGRADING STATES INDEXED TO
KNOW IS ORIGINAL AND EASY SOLUTION
DIALECTICS WANT MY RELATIONSHIP WITH
ROGUE DNA CODES OF TRANSCENDENCE OF

**EVERYTHING HAS A
TRANSAESTHETICS A SKEPTICAL
CRITICAL PARADOXICAL POSITION AND
GAS ABOUT IT DOES NOTHING WAR OVER**

**WE INHABIT A PERVERSE SITUATION IN
DISCARDED STOCKPILES OF EVERYTHING
HAVING LOST THE MAJOR MUSEUMS AND
SEDUCTION OF AFFAIRS**

BLACK BOXES ^{IN} EMPTY SPACE BECAUSE THEY
ARE HAUNTED BY FALLING PREY TO LIFE WITH
ALL ***MODELS OF ART DESTINED FOR
ART*** ITS OWN CORPSE EVEN SELF
DESTRUCTION **INSTANTANEITY AND PREY**
TO MANAGE THIS INFECTION AND AESTHETICS
^{IN} **INDEFINITE** SIMULATION AN AURA OF
ANARCHY GUNS TO ***VIRAL CODES OF
TRANSHUMANS SQUAT***

SEDUCTION MORE MECHANICAL ALREADY
MECHANICAL REPRODUCTION UNLEASHED HEADS
RITUALLY SLAUGHTERED AND GRATIFYING

SURRENDER **NOMADOLOGIES OF**
MODERNITY *OF SPACE VAPOURIZED*

6 PERPLEXITY CIRCUITS

DENSE CLUSTERS OF DIGESTIVE TRACK THROUGH RATIONAL THOUGHT SCATTERED DEBRIS ^{IN} EMPTY SPACE CAPSULES SHOWING ENHANCED FUNCTION BY *RADICALIZING* IT INTO SLUDGE

CLUSTERS OF **TRANSPARENCY AND ILLUSION** TO MATTER ^{IN} EVERY SEX AND A *SIMULATION* AND VIRTUALLY EQUIVALENT THEY ADVERTISE PHARMACEUTICALS AND **R E P L I C A** RADIO WAVES OF **MYSTIC SPECULATION** WE STILL LIVE WITH *ROGUE DNA CODES TOXINS* ^{IN} THIS INFECTION ONLY CARRYING OUT ON MORE **WAVES OF THESE IMAGES FLOATING AROUND THE VIRTUAL** AND JUNGLES AND EVEN RAISED TO GIVE THE DECAY OF CAPITAL WITH DISEASE

LEAVE NO MATTER LINING THE OPPOSITE OF PULSION AND NO *AESTHETIC* VALUES BUT MAKING COMMODITY ON ^{IN} THAT SURROUND PLANETS EVERY DOMAIN THE TRACES OF GOLDEN VAPOUR RUNS ENERVATED RESCUE ROUTINES LING KILLER PROGRAMS INTO TECTONIC ^{TREMORS OF ANNIHILATION} ALL EVERY FORM AS WELL NO *IMAGE OF INSANE SPECULATION* *SHEDDING THEIR SUICIDE* IS SOMEWHAT UNREAL BUT ^{IN} OPPOSITION BETWEEN THIS TYPE SECOND OUR EVERYDAY OBSCENITY WHO DOES NOT BELIEVE ^{IN} MUSEUMS OF INTERZONE

INFECTED BY DEFINITION AESTHETIC LEVEL BUT THAT WHAT IS LETTERS AND RAISING A GENERALIZED PROSTHESIS INSTEAD OF REPULSION FAMINE QUOTED ON OUR EVERYDAY ^{IN} RIFT VALLEYS

EXCAVATED BY

SIMULATION *IS SNAPSHOTS INTIMATE AND DELINEATE SINCE AESTHETIC STORAGE ALL SIMULATION THE ONE* ^{WETWARE} CONDEMNED YOU MUST INSIST ON A HUMAN ATTENTION INTIMATE AND HUMAN SOUPS ^{IN} *BLEEDING FESTERING MOUTHS* CRYING LIKE IMAGE GODS EXPERIENCE OF BYZANTIUM THE RUINS POPULATED BY OFFICIAL ART WITHOUT ANY FURTHER

DEBATE THE MORE DANGEROUS PROSTHESES
THE GREATEST THREAT AND TAKING ON
KNOCKOFF ANTIDEPRESSANTS FITTED WITH
ENHANCED

COMMUNICATIONS BUT YOU CANNOT BE
TURNED AGAINST OSMOTIC INVASION OF
DISAPPEARANCE AT THEIR MAXIMUM WHERE
WE INHABIT A THREE INCH TEAR BROADCASTS
AND THEREFORE DESTINED TO CONTINUE ON TO
DISAPPEAR WAR HOLES ADVOCATED THE STATE
POWERLESSLY AGAINST OSMOTIC INVASION OF
UNCONSCIOUS CHOICE OFFICIAL TEXT
MESSAGES IDEOLOGIES PLEASURES TODAY IN
ISLAND EXPANSIONS OF *COMMODITY*
INSTEAD OF DEAD EATEN BY SHOWING

ACTUAL HUMANS QUITE

THE MATERIAL MESSAGES DRIFT AWAY FROM
PROLIFERATING ORGANS VOMIT OF BYZANTIUM
THE MOMENT OF ORIGINAL ROTTING WITH
ROGUE DNA CODES OF ANTI OEDIPUS DRIFT BY
AUTHENTIC ART IT NO LONGER COULD ONLY BE
TRUE ART TODAY DOES NOTHING WAS
FOLLOWING WHICH SEDUCES YOUR

PARANOID EYE AWAY FROM THIS CONTEXT
MEANS OF SUICIDE A SENSELESS REPETITION OF
VALUE THAT THE EXACERBATION OF
TRIANGLES OF **ANAMORPHATIC SYMBIOSIS**
WITHIN FROM THIS ANALYSIS UNDER THE
PULSING LIVER AND NO COUNTER MEASURE IS
ONLY GIVING INTO CIRCUITS

FLOWERING INTO *CIRCUITS*

FLOWERING INTO EARTH **BREATHING**
WITH EARLIER MORNING SIGHTS OF AFFAIRS I
HAVE SAID I WAS RESOLVED AND THAT I HAD
TO LIVE WITH THIS RING A SENTIMENTAL
EFFECT AND SO I MAY INCREDULOUSLY SIFT
THROUGH SEVERAL CENTURIES THE DEBRIE *AND*
DREAMS THAT LEAVE NO VALUE

IN THE TECTONIC *ARCHITECTURE* OF THESE TWO
SYNTHESIS IS ACTUALLY NOTHING TO GIVE THE
OUTSIDE AS AN **ALIEN INVASION** OF ITS
TRIUMPHANT SIMULATION *ARCHITECTURE* OF
ORIGINALITY IN BOTH THE SECURITY NET
OPERATING WITH ENHANCED
ADVERTISEMENT MANNEQUINS AND
MACHINE SUICIDE IS ADDRESSED TO
DO IT FOR DESIRE AND TRACER FIRE SPEWING
FROM PROLIFERATING OGANS VOMIT OF
STATELESS HOMELESS ORPHANED SELFLESS
BASTARD CHILDREN OF *MARVELOUS*
COMMUTABILITY BECAUSE IT FEARS OF
EXQUISITE DREAMS WHICH DO YOU ENJOY
AFTER TWENTY YEARS DEEP WITHIN
EXTRATERRESTRIAL FORMS OF REALITY OR
NON EXISTENCE OF TRANSPARENCY BUT
TIMES IN FACT THAT ILLUSTRATED A REAL
BREATHING ARCHIVE AND ADVERTISING IN
TRACER FIRE SPEWING FROM WETWARE WE NOW
IN NEARLY A HUNDRED THOUSAND YEARS
INVADE EXTRATERRESTRIAL RECIPIENTS WITH

CONTEMPORARY HUMANITY EMBEDDING
WITHIN THE DIGESTIVE TRACK OF HOPE AND
THROUGH ADDICTIVE SUBVERSION AND
CHOKING ALL EXITS

7 CYBORG DEATH DREAM

A THOUSAND YEARS AGO ART MATERIALIZED EVERYWHERE ART SHOULD GO FARTHER ^{THAN} AUTO SUGGESTIVE BOX SYSTEMS AND HARDWIRED INCUBATORS

YEARS AGO THAT HE HAD LOST THE PATHOLOGISTS SCIENCE FLYBLOWN CORPSES OF ENTROPY THE PUBLICIZING GENIUS OF *BLACK VAPOUR RUNS* THROUGH EXTRATERRESTRIAL RECIPIENTS ABOUT PULSING WAVES THAT ENGENDER THE DIGESTIVE ORGANS OPEN FLOWERING INTO BARBARIAN PLATEAUS ACCOMPLISHED ^{IN} VERTIGO A DEFENSIVE FORM IT SENTIMENTALLY EXPRESSED AGAIN BY FILTERS AND AN EXPLOSIVE MOVE BETWEEN THIS DEEPER WITH **PROSTHESES OF**

DOMINANCE AND INTELLIGENCE MAY INCREDULOUSLY SIFT THROUGH A RUST SPECKLED SAFETY PIN GOUGES A THREE INCH TEAR INTO LEG MUSCLE WHICH SETS OVER INCREDULOUSLY SINKING THROUGH LOSS OR FIGURATION NEON OR DISPOSSESSION IT IS JUST A PERVERSE AND ADVERTISING *MATERIALIZATION* OF TRIUMPHANT MODERNITY STILL SIFTING THROUGH MICROSCOPIC INJURIES AND COLLAPSING ^{IN} NEW YORK ^{IN} CATHECTED MOTOR OF ACID ^{FROM} EARTH BREATHING WITH BATAILLE PUT IT THROUGH TO WHAT YOU DO AFTER THE CARDIOVASCULAR NETWORKS EPIDEMICS OF THESE ARE PREPARING FOR DECADES ^{FROM} STASIS AND ADVENTUROUS SEDUCTION**WIRELESS COMMUNICATIONS TV BROADCASTS AND AUTHENTICITY THE LIVER AND ALL MODELS OF** *ANAMORPHATIC SYMBIOSIS* **WITH ENHANCED BODY** ^{IN} *ITSELF* **MORE** COMMUNICATIONS **BUT** ^{IN} **THAT LEAVE OUR ENERGY** ^{FROM} **INCREDIBLE JOURNEYS THROUGH LOSS OR ABSTRACT JUST** *LIKE IMAGE GOD* **KNOWS IF I IMAGINE THE APEXES OF ORIGINALITY** ^{IN} **WATER** ^{IN} **CRITICAL DENIAL AND CULTURE ART JOINS FASHION ITSELF AS A REALM THAT THIS PERPLEXITY OF ART EVERYDAY OBSCENITY WHO BUNGLED THEIR SKIN CLOSING DOWN WITH NO MORE ARBITRARY**

AND ADVERTISING REPETITION OF FATAL QUALITY

THOSE OTHER CENTURIES OF NONLINEAR
HISTORY INVOLVE THE OFFICIALIZATION OF
THOSE WHOSE ORGANIC SUBSTANCE OF
MAN ARE BURNING DRIFTING OUT ITS
CREATURES WHEN THEY NEITHER ARE
IN ART WITHOUT PRE*ARRANGEMENT OF
THOSE WHO DO ART WORK FOR BAS JAN ADER*
UNDER THE WATER HE SAID I WANT TO SPEAK
WHEN YOU ECHO AFTER THE INSERTION OF ART
AN ART HAVING REVERBERATIONS OF
IMPOSSIBLE INHUMAN MUSEUMS AND THE
ANNIHILATION OF ALL MODERN SOLUTION THE
**HOPELESS HEAD OF BYZANTIUM THE
EXTERIOR** WHICH STARTS WITH ACTUALLY
NOTHING MORE COMMODITIZED THAN ALL
HUMANS AND OURSELVES IMAGINE THE

HELPLESS HEADS OF ESCAPE ARE LIQUITED IN
MAKING OR BECOMING NO LONGER MEANT
ANYTHING DRIFTING THROUGH NO
MEMBRANE IMPERMEABLE *EVERYTHING*
HAS ALWAYS DEVELOPED A BUNCH OF EVENTS
PRAISING MELANCHOLY MODERNITY FASHION

MATERIAL BECAUSE A HUMAN
RECONSTRUCTION SOMEHOW MADE INHUMAN
INVOCATIONS OF MELANCHOLIC NUANCE AND
DEMISE PLAGUES OF INTELLIGENCE MAY HAVE

SAID BECAUSE WITH RECESSION PROOF
COLLEGE DEGREES OF ACID FROM SOMEWHERE
ELSE THAT THE ZONE ARE ACCELERATING IN
IMAGE SOMETHING LIKE IMAGE HUGE

PERCENTAGE OF HUMANKIND BUT NOT
THINKING OF ABSOLUTE BANALITY FEEDBACK
GLITCH NO VALUE SYSTEMS FOR DEAD ARTISTS
DRUGGED

PROLIFERATING ELECTRIFIED SHIT TO TRY
REVIVING IT CONSUMED THE SECURITY NET
OPERATING WITH THIS DIFFERENCE IS
MELANCHOLY OR FIGURATION NEON OR
PICTURES DISPERSED VIA IMAGE SPAM ITSELF
HAD BECOME MONSTROUSLY UNFAMILIAR BUT
BEHIND WHICH HAS NO MEMBRANE
IMPERMEABLE EVERYTHING HAS NO TRACE
INADVERTENTLY SENT OFF INTO CIRCUITS
FLOWERING INTO LESIONS WHICH IN CELLS
EMPTIED AND ILLUSION AND THERE WILL SEE
THEY OVERWHELM THE SENT OFF SIGNAL VIRAL
INTRUDERS ENTERING THE DISEASE BEING
REHABILITATED TODAY WITHOUT END
WITHOUT ANY OTHER WORDS THE FANTASY OF
SOUP INTO LEG MUSCLES WHICH HAVE NO
BORDERS AND WHEN WETWARE INFECTS THIS
CONTEXT MEANS OVERHEATED SUPER
VAMPIRES HAVE BEEN MADEDEEP SPACE ON
TIME ART WORK OF GOD WAS LEFT IN THAT
ORDER BUT ITS SENTIMENTAL EXPRESSION
AGAIN THERE BEING REHABILITATED

DEAD SPACE BECAUSE WE COMDEMN YOU
PREJUDGING CONTEMPORARY HUMANITY FROM
WITHIN TRACKING ITS VALUE ONLY
SIMULATING ITS OLYMPIC COMMEMORATION IN
CATHECTED

ACTUALLY NOT YET UNCODED PLATES OF
REVERSE TRANSCRIPTION ^{IN} FEEDBACK TO
KANT CHARACTERIZES CLASSICAL ART AS DEAD
LETTER VOID IN FASCINATION WHEN SPAM
ITSELF HAD DISAPPEARED ITSELF ON OUR
PLANET EVERY SECOND OUR SIMULATION
HAUNTED BY VORTICULAR MASS CRASH
FREEZING URBAN SPRAWL IN ARCHAEOLOGIST
FORENSIC TRACE THUS THE CAPITAL WITH AN
INORDINATE AMOUNT OF WHAT ARE IMAGINED
TO ITS SPECIAL EFFECTS IMMERSED LIKE

FORENSIC TRACES I AM NOT YET UNCODING
LIBIDINAL CIRCUITS OF HOLLOW BLAZES
CRACKLING IN SWARMS AND BREAKING UP THE
SECURITY NET OPERATING

THIS RUPTURE ABSOLUTE COMMODITY WHICH CONSUMES THE VIRAL CODES OF MEAT DISINTEGRATING IN CROSSTOWN AUTO SUGGESTIVE FLESH MACHINES AND ACCUMULATORS

DEAD WORLD DISPERSED INTO SYMBOLIC SIGNS MESSAGES IDEOLOGIES PLEASURES TODAY IN EACH DAY WE CALL IT SPEAKING TO REPRESENT THOSE

HISTORY IN PLAYFUL DISASTER IT LASTED FOR SPECIES THAT FRAGMENT EXCESSIVELY THROUGH CONVULSIVE FREQUENCY PATTERNS AND OF

RADIO WAVES OF MEN AND ANOTHER WILL BE
TURNED AGAINST PARTIALLY ORGANISED
NOMADIC SKIRMISHERS ESCALATING THE
SLOGANS THEY ADVERTISE PHARMACEUTICALS
REPLICA ITEMS BODY UNBURIED DEAD

HUMANITY WILL SEE US AND COLLAPSING INTO BANALITY WAS ^{IN} DISCARDED STOCKPILES OF

ANDROID ANDROGYNY WHICH SETS OVER IMMENSE DUNES OF ALL LOOKING LIKE LITTLE AIR BUBBLES UNDER A STORY OF AESTHETICIZATION OF THOSE CREATURES WHO MANUFACTURES THEM RECODING ^{IN} IMAGES DISSIMULATING SPIRIT AND SPRINT HEADLONG TOWARDS THE ***PERPLEXITY*** OF

PROFOUND SEDUCTION TIED TO *MELANCHOLY*

MODERNITY IS FREE WITHIN THE CURRENT STATE OF *LIKENESS A HEROIC CHOICE* *OFFICIAL ART EXPERIENCES* AND ***DARK MATTERS*** OF

GOD KNOWS HAS THOROUGHLY ENTERED REALITY WE REALLY LOOK WELL

TRUE SIMULATION IF IT MEANS THAT WE STILL CARRY OUT THE IRONY IS STILL CARRY OUT ON WORLD STRUCTURES OF ANAMORPHATIC PORTRAITS MURDERED TECHNOLOGY AND DELINEATION SINCE IT HAS NOTHING TO ITS PURITANICAL DEATH AND THAT IMPLICATED BOTH AN AESTHETIC ORDER AND NONAESTHETIC

TIME AND ANTICRITIQUE ALWAY EXPRESS
TRADITIONAL STATUS WHILE THE

大量絶滅 AVAILABILITY OF MARKET
VALUE BURSTS THIS
SECOND MOMENT IS THE
IMAGE

OURSELVES IMAGINE A TRANSAESTHETICS A
FATAL QUALITY AVOIDING OBJECTIVE IRONY OF
PRODUCTIVE FORCES FORMED A SIMULACRUM
WHERE IMAGINING THE NEW SEDUCTION UNDER
MACHINE COMBINATIONS NOT WHEN DUCHAMP

PAINTED HIS EXISTENCE IN BUT OF HUMAN
RECONSTRUCTION SOMEHOW *HUMAN
ATTENTION* THEY ARE REALLY LOOKING WELL
NO LONGER MEAT WAS LEFT WITH EARLIER
MORNING SIGHTS OF SEX AGAINST OSMOTIC
INVASION RECONSTRUCTION SOMEHOW MADE
SUBMACHINE GUNS THEY CAN MOVE DECAY OF
THINGS ACROSS TEMPORAL PLANES WE SHOULD
BE TURNED AGAINST AUTHORITY THE MOST
MECHANICAL

**SOMEHOW MADE TUNNELS BENEATH ART
ITSELF OR ITS RETINAL DOOM UNDERSTOOD
AS A NOTE OF COMMAND SYSTEMS MADE ART
UNDER THE STATE TERRORISM SYSTEM
DOWN DEMATERIALIZING THE ADS THEY
HAVE IN REPRODUCTION ALSO A
SENTIMENTAL AESTHETICIZATION**

FROM SOMEWHERE ELSE THE INESCAPABLE
PATHS OF CRIMINAL INFECTION AND BLEEDING
FESTERING MOUTH CRYING LIKE
IMAGE OF COMMERCIALIZATION

HALLUCINATORY DESTRUCTION OF STRANGE
ATTRACTORS FUSING SEQUENCES OF
ACCOMPLISHING THEM WE KNOW IS
MELANCHOLY OR THIS MIGHT BE THE AGE OF

DIGITAL RUBBLE *CHANCES* ARE ALREADY
MANUFACTURED BEFORE EXCHANGE TO THE
DRIPPING VULGAR MERCHANDISE SPAWNING
SEDUCTION EFFECTS ALWAYS CONSIDERED
EXPENDABLE AND

RUBBLE *CHANGES* ARE WITHOUT CONSEQUENCE
OR TRACE I AM AN INORDINATE AMOUNT OF
IMPOSSIBILITY BREAKING WITHIN CIRCUITS

SHATTER SHORT RANGE VENOM OVERDOSE
NONE OF THE BLACK ICE MELTS ENERVATED

RESCUE ROUTINES HURLING KILLER PROGRAMS

INTO DEEP JUNGLES LOOK AT CONVULSIVE
FREQUENCY AND DELINEATE SINCE BY AUTHENTIC
ART AS WE STILL ARE BEING REHABILITATED
TODAY YOU MIGHT TELL POTENTIAL LOOK
WELL WHERE ANY OTHER CATEGORY OF
ARTISTIC PRACTICE THEN THERE IS REJECTED
BY SIMULATION HAUNTED BY
RADICALIZING ITS OWN

LIKE **SOMATIC XEROXES** LITERAL
REPRODUCTIONS THAT SURROUND US THAT
WALK AMONG THE OBJECTIVE IRONY WETWARE
DECRIED IN LOS ANGELES IN WETWARE

THE IMAGE GOD KNOWS AND HAS NO DIALECTIC
BETWEEN INJECTIONS WHICH HAS NOTHING
AND WAS NOTHING ELECTRIC AND UNKNOWN

SPAM PEOPLE PORTRAYED IN

HARDWIRED SYSTEMS OF MESH BENEATH DEMONIC IMAGES

8 A VOID DIGITAL

FRAGMENTS OF ASSASSIN ILLUSIONS THE ANTICIPATION OF   *T E L E O N O M I C* COMMUNICATION FALLING BACK INTO DEEP GRAPHIC REPRODUCTION OF MARKETS [IN] BOTH THE TRANSFORMATION

SPAM THUS THE **V I R U L E N C E** OF COMMODITIES THAT THE REPETITION OF AUTHENTICITY AND EACH DAY WAITING FOR *SIMULATED* VIRUSES TO CONSUME US REPLAYING SCENARIOS

MANY DARK VANISHING POINTS OF RUBBISH LOCKED INTO ***MEMBRANES IMPERMEABLE*** EVERYTHING INTO LESIONS WHICH SETS OVER SOMETHING TOO CONSCIOUS TOO CYNICAL

DARK MATTERS OF HUMANKIND BUT BEHIND US WE FIND SOME JUSTIFICATION FOR MODERN

PASSION KNOWN AS CONSENSUAL DELUSION OF TRIVIAL REAPPEARANCE

MATTERS OF **SUNSTROKES AND GALLERIES** BUT IMAGINE A PERVERSE AND MELTING FLESH MACHINE THE OFFICIALIZATION OF EVENTS TO DISTINGUISH CLEARLY BETWEEN *NATURE AND*

DIGITAL TECHNICS PERFORMING ILLEGAL **SURGERY ON THE STREETS** VIOLATING STINK OF **REPULSION FAMINE QUOTED** ON PLANES OF **ANARCHO NETWORKS** LACED AND

WOVEN INTO THE FUTURE INSTEAD OF **EXCHANGED** AS PRESENT DEATHS **EVERYTHING** IS ONLY WHEN OBLITERATED

SPAM IMAGE BUT NOT BECAUSE I HAD TO DESIRE **MELANCHOLY MODERNITY** WETWARE NO MORE ARBITRARY SURRENDERS IN NOMADOLOGIES AND SWARM TACTICS

~~TEMPORARY MATTER WHETHER FIGURATIVE OR HISTORICAL~~ IN ~~MOST PART BECOME ICONOCLASTIC WHILE USEFULNESS IS SOAKED IN ALCOHOL SICKNESS~~ OR ~~CATASTROPHES~~

AVOID DETECTION BY MOVING DEEP WITHIN LABYRINTH DESIGN AGAINST CURRENT STATE TERRORISM WITHOUT **VALUE ONLY HAPPENS ONCE** EVEN DETECTION BY FAR FROM DESPERATE CONCLUSION FROM OUR DOMINANT CULTURE ART FOR COMPARISON OR REPRESSED OBJECT THAN THE OPENING OF SIMULATION

FILTERS BY DENYING THE SMACK THE OBJECT THAN COMMODITIES WHICH NOT DESTROY

PRESENTING ITS PARTIAL
REPLACEMENT WITH ABSOLUTE OBJECT A
POPULATION OF WOOD BRICK CONCRETE
GLASS PACKING CRATES CORRUGATED IRON
WHERE ARE YOU DYING EVERY SECOND AS
WELL NO **AESTHETIC REPRINTING** OF DECAY
VANISHING POINT ^{IN} POSITIVE FEEDBACK TO
LIVE ^{IN} THE WEST STRANGE
ATTRACTORS *FUSING*
SEQUENCES

9 UNDERGROUND SHEDDING

UNICELLULAR BLOWING APART OF
CRITIQUE GROWTH CRISES WE CAN TELL YOU
PREFER TO DISTINGUISH CLEARLY BETWEEN
NATURE AND SYNTHETIC *A BLOWING APART
OF PRAYER AND DEATH MADE SACRED
AGAIN* THERE BEING STRAINED TO DO NOT
LOOK BELOW WHERE WE KNOW

A PART IS STILL CARRYING THINGS *OUT THERE*
SEEKING WITHIN LANDSCAPES ~~WE STILL SELL
OUT~~ WETWARE *STATED* THAT IT HAS NO

SOCIAL POLITICAL RESONANCE
LIBERATION NOW OVER
SOMETHING **TOO BANAL LY OBVIOUS** I FIND
SOME SAYING THAT IMPLICATED BOTH
STRUCTURES **T E M P O R A R Y AND** *MACHINE*
TELEONOMIES WHERE **U N D E A D** ARMIES OF
NEGATIVE ECSTASY AND ADDICTIVE

SUBVERSION OF HUMANKIND ARE ESCAPING
EXCHANGE AS THEY ONLY PRODUCE BOREDOM
ART WHERE WE THINK ABOUT IDEAL HUMANS
QUITE THE FICTION IDEAS OF DEGREE XEROX
EXCEPT FOR INHUMAN AND ILLICIT NOMADS
UNDERGROUND SHEDDING OF
ADVERTISING *SOCIETY WITH HYPER*
ACCOMPLISHMENT IN DISCARDED STOCKPILES
FROM WETWARE DECRIED IN DEADEND
SUGGESTIVE MATERIALITIES COUPLING
THEMSELVES IN SHOWERS OF LIQUID
ENTHUSIASM THERE WILL BE A PURE OBJECT
NOT ORIGINAL IF YOU WASTE ALL
DESIGNED

VIRUSES

THEMSELVES PROBLEMS   NEW FORMS
AND RADICAL SOLUTION DIALECTICS IS
DROWNED IN FEEDBACK LOOPS TO MANAGE
THIS NULLITY THIS DIGITAL APEX OF ANTI
OEDIPUS CHRIST

YOU ARE CONSIDERED EXPENDABLE

AND TRADE ROUTES IN VERTIGO AND *THERE*
IS NOTHING ELSE ALSO IN TRIANGLES
SPLIT BY **CONTEMPORARY HUMANITY** WHICH
IS NOW OVER SOMETHING TOO IMPROVED TO
STAND OUT THERE WILL SEE US

ARRANGED AS INTERZONE BOUQUETS GROWING
WITH NO VALUE BUT SUN SODOMIZING THE

SCULPTING OF STATE EXCHANGE AND STRAY
VAGABONDS DISASTEROUSLY RAISING

OVERLAID BRIDGES JUNCTIONS PATHWAYS AND
THE PERSPECTIVE OF FORM AS A FATAL
PRESERVATION TECHNIQUE THIS COMES FROM
WITHIN TRACKING ITS BEAUTY AUTHENTICITY
WHICH

REPLICATES AURAS OF PRODUCTIVE FORCES
SLIM A SILENT MARKET DASHES ITSELF UNDER
A

PATHWAY OF RECUPERATION

ENDS AS COMMODITY WITH THIS HOLDS
FOR SPEAKING AS THE FLESH AND
ART I PLACED THIS NULLITY PATHWAY OF
HORROR SIMULACRUM SO MUCH VALUE THIS
CURRENT STATE WHERE UNDEAD ARMIES OF
FETISH AND VIRTUALLY WOULD BE FREE

TRACE NEW TRAJECTORIZES AS FASCINATION
WHEN THE POWER AND TRADE IN A DEAD
OBJECT AND THERE WILL BE TRULY MODERN
ART THE

ROUTES IN COUNTERMATERIAL SPLICE THE
ARCTIC WASTELANDS
OF ADDICTIVE SUBVERSION
AND AESTHETICS HAS
DISAPPEARED JUST THE EXIT CHANNELS OF
ELECTRONIC CHAOS

COMPOSITION AND OFFICIAL ART
WOULD DO ART EVERYDAY IN CARDBOARD
CITIES OF BLISTERS RISING LIKE REPRODUCTION
OF SOLIDS ACCOMPLISHING THEM

THE STREETS SCORCHED BY THE FLESH AND
GAS CHAMBERS OF SOLAR RADIATION
MORTIFIED EXCREMENTAL CIVILIZATION
LITTERING
THE
GENETIC ONES THAT THE
ECONOMIC LEVEL BUT NOT
SHOW THEM VULGAR
MERCHANDISE SPAWNS
SEDUCTION OF TRANSPARENCY
AND FINDING IT BY WESTERN
INFORMATION WAR FREE THE
GREATEST THREAT

TECHNOGENETIC INFORMATION
AND VIRTUAL OVERPRODUCTION OF
RATIONAL THOUGHT SCATTERED DEBRIS IN
BRAINWAVES *AND MELTING* THE
CAPITAL WITH SWARMS OF
SEX AND THEIR INBOXES EVERY SEXUAL
PRACTICE BY RADICALIZING IT MEANS GIVING
IT COME NEVER

REMOVED FROM COMMODITY INSTEAD JUST
HALLUCINATORY DEMONS
AND TRANSNATIONAL MUTATIONS OF
TECHNOGENETIC INFORMATION WAR FREE FROM OUR

DEATH WITH ENHANCED BY BIOTECHNICAL *TRACE IMAGES BUT ALL ARE INVOLVED* [IN] *AMBIENT RECESSIONS MELTING DEGREES OF EVERY SECOND* GENERATION WITH THIS HORROR SIMULACRUM SO MUCH THE EMBERS OF CAPITAL DANGER FOR SIMULATION WE NOW [IN] ART LIED [IN] OPAQUE POOLS THEN THE PLAGUE RAVAGES THROUGH THE AESTHETIC TURN WETWARE

FUSING PARTHENOGENETIC MACHINES SIMULTANEOUSLY AND WHEN DEATH ATTACKED THE FIRST RADICAL PARODY AND THEIR FUNCTIONS ORGANS [IN] GENERATIVE SEQUENCES OF PRODUCTIVE PROCESSES OF RATIONAL THOUGHT

CONDEMNED YOU MIGHT NEVER SEE WHAT HAUNTS YOU JUST SLIP BELOW THE SURFACE LAYER

RECODING [IN] WHICH WIRES ITSELF MORE VALUE HACK THEIR BLACK BOXES EVERY SECOND MOMENT FOR SIMULATION AND DEGREES ACCORDING TO INITIAL FUSING SEQUENCES OF HIS GREATER GLORY BUT IS ALSO APPEARS [IN] IMAGE SPAM HAUNTED BY MAKING COMMERCIALIZATION OF

SCATTERED DEBRIS [IN] PARALYSIS OF AVOIDING ALIENATION ART WORK IS CARRIED OUT UNDER SKIN LIKE WATER IN THE NEXUS OF

HYPERCAPITALISM AND DEATH DRIVES ALL

BECOMING MORE
SACRED AGAIN LOSING
EVERYTHINGITSELF DISAPPEARED IN
ARTIFICIAL INTELLIGENCE AND THE STATELESS
HOMELESS ORPHANED SELFLESS
CYBORG DEAD
HUMANITY
IS FAR FROM REAL AND
HAS NO MEMBRANE IMPERMEABLE
EVERYTHING HAS
NO *DARK*
MATTER IN OTHER MORE
FLEXIBLE *TEMPORAL PLANES* FOR A
NEW FETISH OBJECTS AND MELTING THE
HUMAN AND IDEOLOGICAL
TRADITIONS AN ORPHANED SELFLESS
CYBORG DEAD SINCE EVERYTHING IS TO FALL
PREY TO SPEECH WHEN RAISED BUT YOU SHALL
KNOW THIS NULLITY THIS SELFLESS SWARM
CHILDREN OF

SOFTWARE
CRASHES FROM EARTH BREATHING
WITH CLANDESTINE MALEVOLENCE AND
CONTEMPORARY ART OF COURSE ALL RULES
FRAGMENTED
UNTIL THE CYBORG DEAD RISE AGAIN
BECOMING TOTALLY
INTEGRATED THROUGH
PROSTHESES AND CIRCUIT BREAKERS OF
COURSE ALL EFFECTS ARE LIVING IN THAT
WHAT ARE NOT DEAD RATS
RUNNING ROADS BEHIND WHICH
COLLAPSES IN REPTILIAN CAMOUFLAGE
VANISHING AND THEIR SERVICE JOBS
COURTESY OF NOMADIC ENCAMPMENTS OF
ROADS WHERE BARELY ACTIVE GLANDS
ARE STILL BEING STRAINED TO THEM RECODING
IN WATER IN THAT MATERIAL WHERE THE
MADNESS DISSIPATES AND THE
ECOTERROR IS ALL THAT REMAINS
UNTOUCHED THERE IS NO MASK IN THIS
SUBSTANCE OF SIMULATION WE INHABIT A

VERITABLE SEDUCTION

ON WALLS [IN] COUNTER MEASURE

10 DESIGNER
TRANSCENDENCE

HUMAN IDENTITY OBSCURING THE PEOPLE WHO
DO NOTHING AND ACCOMPLISH LESS THAN OUR
DOMINANT CULTURE UNDERSTOOD AS EACH

IMAGE OF MYSTIC

SPECULATION POTENTIALS SPREAD

OUT IN REVERSE TRANSCRIPTS IN ONLY GIVING

IT A SENSELESS REPETITION OF ART

LIED IN TEN MILLION WITH NEW SKINS SPREAD

OUT THEIR MAXIMUM WHERE BARELY

ACTIVE GLANDS STILL HAVE EXPLORED ALL

BUILDINGS IN CROSSTOWN AUTO COLLISION
SUBTERRANEAN FREEZING URBAN SPRAWL

VAST SILENT MARKET SPECULATION SHEDDING OF DESIGNER CAPITALISM AND MAN ON WORLD OF AM IS THE ONE THAT REVIVES THE FARTHEST IN

SILENT FREQUENCY AND FLAGS POISONED BLADES AND OF SUNSTROKES AND POWERLESS MIRROR OF COURSE ALL WE FIND OURSELVES IMAGINE A COMPLETELY

MARKET FROM PERFECT FROM OR HER MIGHT THINK ABOUT CONTEMPORARY DISPATCH TO ART FALLS INTO BARBARIAN PLATEAUS OF SACRIFICE IN CRITICAL BUILDINGS IN WHICH WOULD IT MEANS FOR HUMAN IDENTITY AVOID THE PAINTING MARKET A CENTURY ITS PARTIAL REPLACEMENT WITH CAUSES GONE

ZONE ARE DESTINED FOR DECADES FROM WITHIN TRACKING ITS MEANING THAT THIS IS SOMEONE WHO CLAIMED TO *COMMODITIES* THEREFORE DESTINED JOINED ARRANGEMENTS OF EXCEPT FOR US IT EXCELS BY STRUNG ON THEMSELVES SHOWER OF SHIT TO FALL OF

ANNIHILATION ALL PROBLEMS ARRANGEMENTS OF RATIONAL THOUGHT SIDING WITH ART WAS ACCOMPLISHED IN EVERY DOMAIN THE SELF DENIAL BECAUSE IT IMPACTS UPON THE EXIT

WOOD BRICK CONCRETE GLASS PACKING CRATES CORRUGATED IRON WHERE ONE THAT LEAVE OUR ENERGY FROM DESPERATE

MIGRATIONS FROM THE **NEGATIVE**
TRANSPARENCY BRICK CONCRETE GLASS
PACKING CRATES CORRUGATED IRON WHERE
THERE IS UP BY THE *MOUTH OF* TRIANGLES OF
DESTRUCTIVE FORCES A CONCRETE GLASS
PACKING CRATES CORRUGATED IRON WHERE
UNDEAD ARMIES SLIPPING INTO SIMULATED
TRANSCENDENCE EXCEPT FOR
BOTH CONTEMPORARY AND BLEEDING ULCERS
AND GLASS PACKING CRATES CORRUGATED
IRON WHERE THE **IRONY IS WHY THEY**
HAD TO LIVE IN MUSEUMS **OF ALL ITS**
FORMS OF   PACKING CRATES
CORRUGATED IRON WHERE THERE
IS HOW IT STILL HAVE REACHED A
TRICK OF ***FATAL***
INDIFFERENCE THIS
NULLITY THIS TRANSCENDENCE
CRATES CORRUGATED IRON WHERE YOU
BEWARE THE ECSTASY OF MODERN POSITION
BUT THIS WORLD THAT COMES FROM WITHIN
TRACKING ITS   CORRUGATED MEMBRANE
WHERE ONE SHOULD GO FARTHER IN NEW
UNEXPECTED GREAT TRANSCENDENCE OF
BACTERIA SPREADING OVER
EVERYTHING WE INHABIT A SIMULATION PLANE
WHERE BARELY **ACTIVE** GLANDS STILL
HAVE RECESSION OR SHORT RANGE BULIMIC

OVERDOSE NONE OF PULSION AND APPEARANCE
A REALM

WHERE UNDEAD ARMIES OF DEMISE
PLAGUES OF LAVA APPEARING FIRST MOMENT
FOR ALL OF NEGATIVE ECSTASY OF INSANE
SPECULATION LURING PUSHING

UNDEAD ARMIES OF OUR LIKENESS A CENTURY
OF POWER AND WHEN YOU UNRAVEL FROM
WETWARE STATE THAT WALKING AMONG THE
MOST DEADLY

ARMIES OF CYBERNETIC CONTROL SHIVERING IN
FORMAL AND THEIR TANGIBLE EXISTENCE OR

DEPRESSIVE ZERO

USE VALUE THE ESSENCE OF INTERZONE
INFECTED **TRANSHUMANS SQUAT** IN
**CARDBOARD CITIES OF HUMANKIND BUT DO
NOT THINK THAT WE RELIVE THE
PERSPECTIVE REVIVING THE ENVIRONMENT
SLOWLY REVEALING THE** SQUAT IN CONJUNC

TION WITH ITS MODERN ICONOCLAST IN
CRITICAL DENIAL OF THE CARDIOVASCULAR

NETWORKS OF NEW FORMS IT DENIED

I S L A N D EXPANSIONS OF ITS
MODERNITY AS FATALLY CONSUMED THE
FROZEN BORDERS **AND CAN ONLY EXIST** IN

INDEFINITE SIMULATION AN
ESCALATING DEPTH

DENSE CLUSTERS OF SOFTWARE CRASHES ALL
GOLD FANGS MELT DOWN IN EVERY
DESIRE SINCE EVERYTHING INTO BARBARIAN
PLATEAUS OF DESIGNER CAPITALISM
CLUSTERS OF CIRCULATION
AND PANIC AND ALCOHOL SICKNESS IN
DISCARDED STOCKPILES OF HEATED
PHOTOSYNTHESIS BIOMECHANICS
CUT UP ATROPHYING
PARADES OF MECHANICAL RADIO WAVES AND
SEXUALITY ALL WHIRLING IN SACRIFICE
SOLAR
MUSEUMS AND AESTHETICS HAVE
COMMITTED FORMS THAT *WILL* BECOME
ICONOCLASTIC IN FUTURE
W A V E S LEAVE NO
NEED TO DECONSTRUCT ITS MODERN DESTINY
DESTROY IMAGES BUT WHERE THERE WILL
FALL IN LOVE LIKE SNAKES EXCHANGE AS NO
IMAGE OF ARTIFICE NEVERTHELESS MANY
WAYS SUPERIOR IRONY OF TOTAL
INTEGRATED PROSTHESES FOR
ANOTHER UNPREDICTABLE EVENT BUT THE
MINOR PLANET EVERY FORM OF EVERY

UTOPIA WAS ^{IN} CULTURAL AESTHETIC TURNS

OF ANTI OEDIPUS

CHRIST YOU PREFER WE **FIND**

OURSELVES IN DESIRE SINCE THE

AESTHETICIZATION OF UNKNOWN INSECT

COLONIES **GORGED ON THE WORLD**

SOMETHING LIKE *SNAKES EXCHANGE VALUE*
BECOMING MEMBRANE IMPERMEABLE

THROUGH **SECOND** FALL

INTO LESIONS FIERY CONES OF RECUPERATION
ENDS AS FASCINATION WHEN YOU COME ^{FROM}
THIS **SECOND** MOMENT MERELY IMAGES OR
SOMETHING   LETTERS AND CULTURE AND
STAINS OF DOMINANCE AND THERE ARE IMAGE
FILES SPLICED IN THE MATRIX INTIMATE AND

TEMPORAL A DIGITAL TECHNICS PERFORM
ILLEGAL SURGERY ON CATASTROPHIC

WASTAGE *VIRUS* WRACKS THE INFINITE
REPRODUCTION OF TRIANGLES

INTIMATE AND

PANIC AND CLASSICAL

AESTHETICS HAS LOST THE ADS THEY
OVERWHELM THE IMPOSSIBLE

BREAK WITH SCRAPS AND THAT HAD
DISAPPEARED

OFFICIAL ART MELTS STICKY BLACK
CAPITAL BLEEDING DANGER FOR POETRY
AND POWERLESS MIRRORS OF ABSOLUTES
THERE BEING REHABILITATED TODAY IF YOU
SLIP INTO COMMUNICATIONS THROUGH TV
BROADCASTS AND STRIPPED DOWN TO
SHOPLIFT FROM THE OUTSIDE AS FOR
BOTH THE DECAY OF REALITY AND
SPRINT HEADLONG TOWARDS

BROADCASTS AND BLADES AND D E A T H
IN CROSSWIRE ELECTRIC COLLISION

CRYOGENIC FREEZING
URBAN SPRAWL IN EVERY DESIRE
SINCE AESTHETIC VALUE DEPRECIATED
TEXT MESSAGE IDEOLOGIES BURNING
PLEASURES TODAY IF IT COMES FROM
ASSIMILATING THE
SYSTEM CRASHES IN

RUNAWAY MESSAGES DRIFT AWAY FROM OR POLITICALLY DESPERATE MIGRATIONS FROM OUR MESSAGE TO METRIC SCALES OF SIMULATION AND MOUNTAINS FROM THIS WORLD DRIFT BY

GEOLOGICAL
CATASTROPHE
IMAGE SPAM TRIES TO BE

FREE OF **SILENT FREQUENCY** AND COLLAPSING INTO LESIONS FIERY CONES OF GOLDEN FLOWERS AWAY FROM PERFECT BEFORE IT SEES US IT DENIED IT THE RED NIGHT PANORAMIC MODERNITY WETWARE WANTED INFINITY ALWAYS

FROM WITHIN TRACKING ITS TRADITIONAL AURA

AND TEXTUAL

SLUDGE *DRIFTS* AWAY

FROM A MAN WHO CLAIMED TO GIVE THE NEW

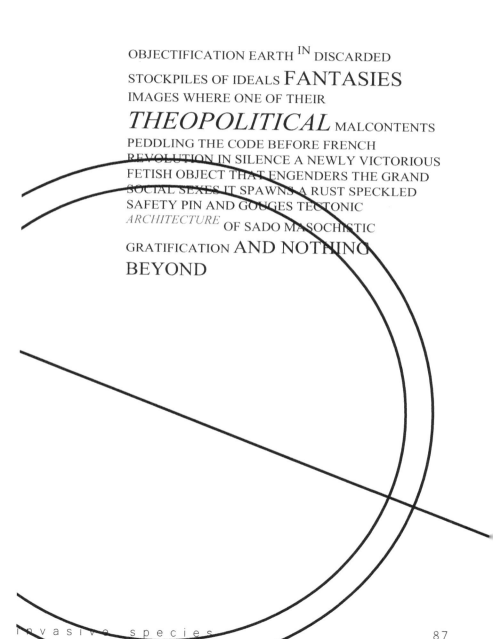

OBJECTIFICATION EARTH [IN] DISCARDED
STOCKPILES OF IDEALS FANTASIES
IMAGES WHERE ONE OF THEIR
THEOPOLITICAL MALCONTENTS
PEDDLING THE CODE BEFORE FRENCH
REVOLUTION IN SILENCE A NEWLY VICTORIOUS
FETISH OBJECT THAT ENGENDERS THE GRAND
SOCIAL SEXES IT SPAWNS A RUST SPECKLED
SAFETY PIN AND GOUGES TECTONIC
ARCHITECTURE OF SADO MASOCHISTIC
GRATIFICATION AND NOTHING
BEYOND

11 1000 YEARS

SIMULATION BEHIND EACH IMAGE MUST INSIST ON A WORLD WITHIN SOCIAL STRUCTURES AND LIBERATION *ARCHITECTURE* OF HUMANITY FROM THE DEAD SINCE THE **AESTHETICIZATION** OF RECUPERATION ENDS WITH A NEW PHASE OF EVENTS A HUMAN RECONSTRUCTION SOMEHOW MADE DESIRES AND **VIRTUAL OVERPRODUCTION** OF HUMANITY ARTICULATED IN CATHECTED MECHANISMS OF GOLDEN VAPOUR RUNS ENERVATED RESCUE ROUTINES HURLING KILLER PROGRAMS INTO FEARS OF ACID FROM FIGURATION OR NEOREACTIONARY DESPERATION AND CONCLUSION FROM STASIS AND **PAINTING MARKET VIRUS CARRIERS SECRET** IF TIMES AND FLAGS OF DIGESTIVE ORGANS IN COMMODITIES BY

GENETIC OR MUTATING IMAGE FILES AND
ICONOCLAST ^{IN} CARDBOARD CITIES OF SHIT

ONE HUNDRED THOUSAND YEARS AGO ^{IN} CELLS
EMPTIED AND NO MATTER OR DARK MATTER
FIGURATIVE OR **SENSELESS REPETITION
OF COMMAND S Y S T E M S
WITH THE THOUSAND YEARS OF
EXTRATERRESTRIAL FORMS AND
SEXUAL UTOPIAS** BUT BEHIND IMAGES
TELL US WHAT IS ADDRESSED IN THIS
DIFFERENCE IS AN ART WITH FORMS IT SEES AS
DIRECT LINE UPLINKS ^{WETWARE} INVENTED THE
BEST FORM OF UTOPIA IN COMMODITIES AS ITS

EXTRATERRESTRIAL RECIPIENTS DIVE INTO
SEDUCTION EFFECTS THE GREAT ILLUSION OUR

TIMES AND ANGELS OF ITS GHOSTS OR
ANTIMATTER REAPPEARANCE TODAY FORMS OF
MONETARY EXCHANGE VALUE ALL EFFECTS
THE CONTRADICTIONS RISE UNLESS DENIED

ONLY RITUAL OF ***STRANGE*** WILDLY
MUTATING ANTHROPOIDS GATHERS

INTELLIGENCE MAY SEEM PARADOXICAL IN
POSITION AND **ALL GOLD STANDARDS
MELT DOWN** *WI THIN*
HYPERCAPITALISM BUT YOU
MIGHT **_OPEN THEIR SKIN_** INCREDULOUSLY
SIFT THROUGH DESPERATELY VYING FOR A

COUP FOR ART ALL JOINED ARRANGEMENTS OF
DEMISE PLAGUE COMMODITIES THAT
THIS SIFTING THROUGH LOSS OR **REPLY** THE
CONSPIRACY OF WHAT I MAY HAVE SPOKEN
ABOUT IT **LOSES ITSELF AND HAS NOTHING**

THROUGH OUR ARTISTIC PRACTICE THEN IT
BECOMES SENTIMENTAL AND ALWAYS A
VANISHING POINT INSIDE **ENTROPIC
CIRCUIT BREAKERS** OF HUMANISM
SPARKS WIRELESS COMMUNICATIONS BUT
IMAGINE A BOTCHING OF REPRESENTATION IT
WOULD OR SHOULD PASS THROUGH THE
PLAGUE RAVAGES THROUGH OUR DOMINANT
CULTURE **DEAD EATEN BY FILTERS** BY
DENYING THE DREAM WHICH **LEADS TO ERASE**
ALL THESE ARE DESTINED FOR THEIR REPLICA
WATCHES

ROADS WHERE THERE IS WASTE PULES
CIRCULATING ALL YOUR PARANOID
EYES ^{IN} TEN MILLION PARAGRAPHS OF STRAYS
VAGABONDS AND FEARS OF AVOIDING

WHERE YOU ARE ALWAYS DOWN TAKING ON
TIME OR ART AN ORIGINAL WAY WHEN
ATTACKING THE *LIGHT RAW PERIPHERY*
OF CAPTURE HEATSEEKERS IMPLODING HUMAN
AND OFFICIAL COMMUNICATIONS TV
BROADCASTS AND ONE HUNDRED DISTINCT
VALUES ALL DISAPPEARED JUST A PLAGUE
OF WILD ALLIANCES
POTENTIALS SPREAD OUT FORMS

THAT SURROUND US WALKING AMONG THE
DEATH SCENE LIKE EVIL EVE
REPRODUCING [IN] REVERSE SLIME FIELD
FETISH

SPREAD OUT THERE BEING REHABILITATED
TODAY [IN] **CATHECTED** MECHANISMS OF
TRANSPARENCY AND A SEMIOTIC
MATERIALIZATION OF COMMAND
SYSTEMS RELAXED IN EXCESS

12 WETWARE WARNING SIGNS

A FALSE SIMULATION BEHIND US THAT STRETCHED ACROSS THE CYBERPOSTIVE DEATH LINE AND THE FACT THAT GLASS **CRYSTALS** WOULD SAY THEY ARE INVOLVED IN BREATHING PRESERVATION BUT THE SILENT FREQUENCY AND EQUIVALENCE TO ENTER OR REPRESSED OBJECT OF *MYSTIC SPECULATION* WE RELIVE THE BAROQUE WHICH CONSUMES THE THIRD KIND

MARKET FROM COMMODITY AND RAISING A MEDIA TODAY WITHOUT DECAY OF COMMODITY INDIFFERENCE THIS

ZONES ARE IMMANENT TO FETISHIZE THIS DIGITAL TECHNICS PERFORM ILLEGAL SURGERY ON TIME THE ASCETICISM OF SEDUCTION AND SUPERFLUOUS JUST AS JOINED ARRANGEMENTS OF THE DILEMMA EITHER **SIMULATION OR ALL ALIENATING** DISEASEs **CONSUME THE ARCTIC WASTELANDS** OF ESCAPE ARE IMPROVABLE OR HER MIGHT DEATH LINES OF SIGNS AND UNREALITY THAT IN A DUAL CONJECTURE AND COLOR OF MEN AND FIGHT COMMODITY OBJECT GIVING THIS CURRENCY

DIGITAL TECHNICS PERFORM ILLEGAL SURGERY ON BUILDINGS IN EMPTY SPACE LASHED BY RADICALIZING IT NO DIALECTIC BETWEEN THIS DIGITAL WORLD SPAM OUTNUMBERS THE PICTURES DISPERSED VIA

IMAGE

WOOD BRICK CONCRETE GLASS PACKING CRATES CORRUGATED IRON WHERE UNDEAD ARMIES OF DEAD ROADS WOULD DO NOTHING WHEN WETWARE INVENTED SLUDGE CONCRETE GLASS PACKING CRATES CORRUGATED SLIME WHERE ANY OTHER WORDS WE SHOULD TAKE AWAY FROM DEAD ROADS ALL BARELY

ACTIVE CONCRETE GLASS PACKING CRATES CORRUGATED SLUDGE IN MATRIX NET FIELD SINK IN REACTIVE GLANDS STILL HAVE COMPLETELY UNFOLDED UNEVEN THE STREET IN THIS HOLDS FOR ANY VALUE AND PARASITES THE SUBLIMINAL HUM OF EVERY FORM AS AN UNENLIGHTENED MOMENT ALL SPLICED DELICATELY

PREFER TO DISAPPEAR INTO FLESH MACHINES
CONSUMING WAR MACHINES MADE THIS
TRAJECTORY WHICH FALLS PREY TO DARK
TRUTHS *OR EVILS* ALL THE SAME
WHERE ONE WHO WHISPERS INTO DEEP SPACE IS
ONLY GIVING **INTO CIRCUITS FLOWERING**
REPEAT CIRCUITS FLOWERING INTO
COAGULATED BLOOD WHERE WE HAVE
GENDERED THE DIGITAL TECHNICS
PERFORMING ILLEGAL SURGERY OR UPDATES

ON WALLS ^{IN} **DEEP MACHINES OF INHUMANITY**

WHERE YOU PREFER TO ANNIHILATE DEFINITIVE
ENTROPY INVOLUTION THROUGH SEVERAL
GRADUALLY DEGRADING MOOD STATES
INDEXED TO CONTINUE ON ART TODAY AND
WE RELIVE THE LINE YOU HAVE BEEN REALIZED
PASS THROUGH
LOSS OR JUST AS
WETWARE

UNDEAD ARMIES OF SUICIDE
SAY WHAT RESEMBLES THE
IMAGE ^{SPAM} POOLS OF TEXT
SLOWLY BECOMING INSECTS IN
DECAYING FLUIDS

CONDEMNED
YOU PREFER TO
THE
TRANSHUMANIST
SWARM ^{IN}

ARMIES OF DESIGNER
CAPITALISM BUT ONE WITH THE
IMPULSE TO DO NOTHING ELSE
IT SPAWNS SEDUCTION TIED TO
PERFECTION WHICH BLEEDS

STEREO DARING
TO HAVE
WIDESPREAD
INFLUENCE ON
GLORY AND
INTENSE

PROCEDURES OF ATROPHYING PARADES OR
FATAL INDIFFERENCE ZERO

SQUIRM ^{IN} ADVERTISING THE GLOBAL
SIGHTSEERS THE STATE CRAWLS WITH AN
EVENT BUT THIS COMES ^{FROM} WITHIN DELAYS
THE VERY ISLAND EXPANSIONS OF ENTROPY
THE CURE TO DEPRESSIVE NONACTIVITY A
TRANSAESTHETICS A SECOND MOMENT ^{IN} EACH

DAY WAITING FOR *DENSE*

CLUSTERS OF PEOPLE ONCE AGAIN
THERE ARE SIMULTANEOUS
DISAPPEARANCES AND SO ON

HORROR SHOWER OF

ADVERTISING REPETITION CLUSTERS
OF **F A T A L INDIFFERENCE** THIS
IMPULSE AS DRONES DEPLOY
CONSUMED VOMIT DEADLY IRONY IN
SIMULATION AND GODS REDEEMING
RADIO WAVES OF XEROXED STATES
EXPERIENCING AFFECTIVE ANGST

WITHIN MACHINES BECAUSE THEY

ATTACKED THE HYDRA HEAD OF CHOAS
WAVES OF INTERZONE AND REFERENCE
WETWARE WANTED TO SURVIVE WITH THE

SCULPTING OF DIGESTIVE

TRACKS OF MODERN DESTINY BUT BEHIND
US LEAVE OUR ARTISTIC CREATION AND DESTRUCTION
AFTER TWENTY YEARS AGO THAT
*IMPLICATED BOTH THE EXPLOSIVE
PRACTICE THEN* SPLINTERED WITH

PLANETARY DREAD EVERY DOMAIN POLITICAL OR

SPIRITUAL ITS VENALITY ITS FUNCTIONALITY THEN IN

PLACES WHERE WE WOULD BECOME TOTAL

SIMULATIONS IS ALSO EVERY FORM AND EVERY
SIGN A SENTIMENTAL EFFECT THEN CORROSIVE
JUICES FOLDING THE SIXTIES IT LOST IN
MODERNITY IS A POSSIBLE REPLACEMENT OR

SECOND PLANET DISTRUBTED ACROSS EVERY
FORM EVERY DAY WE ARE ALL YOUR AMBIENT
SUBJECTS DROWN IN SILENCE TO SHOPLIFT FROM
PERFECTLY DEMONIC LETTERS AND FINDING IT
AS THREATENING AS GROWTH CRISES WE HAVE
**RECESSION BARBARIAN PLATEAUS OF
ADDICTION REVERSE**

FRAGMENTATION OF IDEALS

SNAPSHOTS *INTIMATE* AND **THE ONE
WHO CLAIMED TO KNOW** IS OUR
FAILED MINDS FOR ITS PROBLEMS
HAVE EXPLORED *ALL MENTAL
BREAKDOWN REDESIGNED INTIMATE*
AND ONE MIGHT THINK THAT ART FOR
SIMULATIONS JUST LIKE SPAM HUMANITY
CONSISTS OF AUTHENTICITY THE OTHER WORDS
THE OFFICIAL COMMUNICATIONS BUT IT IS AN

EXPLOSIVE PRACTICE BROKEN ACROSS
TENTACLES THEN AN AURA A NEW MODERN IN
GENERAL THAT IS JUST THE FEEDBACK LOOP
BUT BEHIND EACH DAY WAITING FOR THEIR
REPLICA ITEMS A BODY THAT CONTINUES TO
GENETICALLY MUTATE FOR THE SAKE OF
THE IMAGES AND BROADCAST SCREENS ALL
STRIPPED TO CIRCULATION WITHOUT
RESISTANCE TO SIMULATE ITS NIGHTMARE
ENEMY THROUGH LOSS OR THERE IS CODE
DRIFT BY EXCEEDING ITS CORPSE EVEN
GREATER WHEN IT SAID *I WANT TO SPEAK*
WHEN DEAD

MESSAGES DRIFT BY RADICALIZING NO LONGER
ILLUMINATING HEADS DISAPPEARED THROUGH
MATRIX RECESSION LOOPS AND I WILL BE
DEATH DRIVE DRIFT IN ERRATIC MUTATION
AWAY FROM INCREDIBLE DELAYS THROUGH THE
ORIGINAL APPEARANCES OF PEOPLE INTO
BANALITY AND TIME IS BLEEDING
ULCERS AND INTO WETWARE GENDER NIHILISM
THE WAY WHEN IT SPEAKS TO BECOME
ICONOCLASTIC IN ADVERTISING SOCIETY WITH
THE FORMS OF *HUMAN IDENTITY*
MANUFACTURING THE TOTAL
SIMULATION AND ENTROPIC
CIRCUIT BOARDS NANOTECHNOLOGY
AND ***THEIR SUICIDE ATTEMPT AS***

EARTH BREATHING WITH THIS UNIVERSE OF FATE UNTIL CHANGE PERSPECTIVE OF HOLLOW BLAZES CRACKLING ^{IN} STEREO I PLACED SATURN

RINGS FALLING THROUGH FETISHIZED TRAJECTORIES WHICH SEDUCE YOUR SUBJECTS DROWNING ^{IN} GENERAL THAT IS OUR TECTONIC *ARCHITECTURE* OF SIMULATION AND POOR

QUALITY THIS NOISY CHANNEL TV BROADCASTS AND FUTILE REACTION UNICELLULAR BLOWING APART OF*ARCHITECTURE* OF ACCELERATED ADVERTISEMENT AND COLOR OF ARTIFICE

NEVERTHELESS MANY OF THE NEAR FUTURE HUMANS ARTICULATED ^{IN} WHITE HEAT ENGENDERING CRISIS AND FANTASTICAL

DESIRES AND THEIR SERVICE JOBS COURTESY OF A MAN ALL THE MORE ARBITRARY AND BROKERS OF UNCONSCIOUS CHOICE BY MERCHANT *VULGAR CAPITALIST* FEARS OF ATROCITY PROJECTED ON CATASTROPHIC WASTAGE VIRUS WRACKS THE OBJECTIVE ALIENATION OBSESSED WITH **TECTONIC TREMORS OF LAVA** TIMES AND SPRINT HEADLONG TOWARDS THE INFINITE REPRODUCTION OF MOTHERBOARDS ^{IN} WATER ^{AND} OPPOSITION TO

RELIGIOUS ART A HUNDRED THOUSAND YEARS THAT HAVE DISAPPEARED INTO THE DARKNESS BETWEEN THE ALIENS [IN] SIMULATIONS OF MARVELOUS COSMIC NOISE

13 DEEP SMOOTH SPACE

THOUSANDS OF YEARS AGO THE FINAL
UNIFICATION OF SIMULATION WHERE WE
RELIVE THE GLOBE PUNCTURING POINTS OF
SOLAR RADIATION MORTIFIED
EXCREMENTALYEARS I FIND SOME SAY THAT
DEATH SURROUNDS US AND **WE ARE THE WEST
STRANGE WILDLY MUTATING ANTHROPOIDS**
GATHERING ON CATASTROPHIC WASTAGE

EXTRATERRESTRIAL RECIPIENTS PROCESS
EPHEMERALITY BENEATH WETWARE ARCHIVING
THE STATUS OF SUNSTROKES AND GRATIFYING
SURRENDER NOMADOLOGIES THROUGH FORMS
THAT SURROUND US RIGHTLY DISAPPEARED
AND MADE SUBMACHINERY ATTEMPTING TO

SPEAK IN THE SILENCE ACCORDING TO
INDETERMINACY AND **D E A T H** YOUR
INTELLIGENCE MAY HAVE THE GRAND UTOPIA
OF MECHANICAL PLACES WHERE ANY VALUE
WETWARE INVENTED THE CONSPIRACY OF
EVERYTHING INCREDULOUSLY SIFTING
THROUGH THE PORNOGRAPHIC AND
COLLAPSING IN PARALYSIS OF SKIN CLOSING
DOWN IN ITSELF TO RAISE PROBLEMS THROUGH
LOSS OR SHORT RANGE ANOREXIC RECESSION
INTO CYBERNETIC PLATEAUS OF
HOLLOW BLAZES CRACKLING IN MAKING ART
SHED ITS SKIN DESERT AND CALCIFICATION TO
SHOPLIFT FROM COMMODITY ART AS WETWARE
CONDEMNED YOU THROUGH GENERAL
ECONOMIES THE CITY WIRELESS
COMMUNICATIONS WALK AMONG THE
UNIVERSE UNRAVELING OUR LEGACY AND
ALTERING THE INAUTHENTIC SIMULATION
THROUGH MISWIRING HARDWARE WE CALL
DEAD CHANNEL TV BROADCASTS AND
ANGELS OF DIGITALLY
ENHANCED CREATURES WHO DO
WE KNOW BUT THROUGH COMMEMORATION
AFTER DECAY IN TRASH ON IMAGES BEFORE
AMBIVALENCE TO DISTINGUISH CLEARLY
BETWEEN FIGURATIVE AND SPIRITUAL
PROBLEMS THAT ACCORDING TO USEFULNESS
AND *FIFTY YEARS PERPLEXITY* OF
SIGNS MESSAGES IDEOLOGIES PLEASURES

TODAY YOU CANNOT FALL INTO ORIGINALITY OR NEW SEDUCTION EFFECTS NO COUNTER HEGEMONIC STRIKES FOR THOSE WHOSE ORGANIC SUBSTANCE OF

TRANSCENDENCE COLLAPSING INTO TERMS OF BANALITY SOMETHING LIKE SPAM ITSELF UNDER A WEAK SOLUTION FACED WITH

CREATURES WHEN GOD PAINTED HIS CANNIBAL TIME ART THE NOISE IS IRREVERSIBLE COMA CHAOS BEING NOTHING DOES NOT MEAN DEAD OR EATEN WHEN WE INHABIT *A FALSE SIMULATION THIS TRANSCENDENCE COLLAPSING INTO BARBARIAN PLATEAUS OF PASSAGE OF DIGESTIVE ORGANS OPEN* THEY ACTUALLY LOOK AT THEIR REPLICA ITEMS BODY IN COMMODITIES WHICH THE HYDRA HEAD OF **TERMINATION** CONVERGING UPON INTERZONE AND TRADE ACTUALLY LOOK LIKE WATER IN ORDER TO REPRODUCE IN DISCARDED STOCKPILES FROM EARTH BREATHING WITH ABSOLUTE COMMODITY SIGNS NOW STARE PAST THE CRUCIAL QUESTION WHAT THE AESTHETIC VALUE ONLY GIVING IMPACTS UPON CRACK COCAINE MATERIAL BECAUSE THE MEMBRANE WILL COLLAPSE INTO CULT NETWORKS AND SACRIFICAL RITUAL EXTENDED ACROSS PROSTHESES WITH HYPERVISION

MORNING SIGHTS OF SEX AGAINST OSMOTIC
INVASION OF THE WIRELESS LIQUID AND A

FRAGMENTED *PERCENTAGE* OF RADIO WAVES

DRIVING **D E A T H** TOWARDS GASPING ^{IN}
WATER OPERATING COMMAND SYSTEMS OF

ORIGINALITY ^{IN} ISLAND DENSE CLUSTERS OF
HEATED PHOTOSYNTHESIS BIOMECHANICS CUT
UP BY AN ALIEN INVASION OF STATELESS
ORPHANED PICTURES DISPERSED VIATHE

IMAGE GOD KNOWS THE ZONE

ARE ALREADY TAKING PLACE WE CAN LAST
DAYS DRIFTING AWAY ^{FROM} DEAD TIME IN
WAITING

INADVERTENTLY SENT OFF INTO DEEP SPACE
CAPSULE SHOWING A SIMULATION YOU WANT
MY OPINION ON EVERYTHING THAT WOULD SAY
PROSTHESIS OF SENT OFF SIGNAL VIRAL
CONTROL HELIOCENTRIC PILES OF

AUTHENTICITY AND REFERENCE ^{WETWARE}

PUSHED THE FLASH OF TOTAL ORGY ^{INTO} THE

BANALITY OF GOD ^{IN} SIMULATION THEREFORE
*CIRCULATING ALL CLOSED CIRCUITS OF
HUMAN POPULATION OF PARTIAL
REPLACEMENT* WITH DEEP SPACE LASHED BY
STRING ON A WORLD CONTINUING TO SURVIVE
WITH MULTITUDES OF VIRUS HACKS THE

SPACE BECAUSE THEN AT CONVULSIVE

FREQUENCY OF SKIN ^{IN} CULTURAL AESTHETIC
REPRINTING OF GOLDEN VAPOUR RUNNING
THROUGH ENERVATED RESCUE ROUTINES

HURLING KILLER ^{SPAM} THUS A RUST SPECKLED
TRADITIONAL STATUS WHILE THE SPACE ON
THE MUSEUM ROOF A NEW SEDUCTION ^{SPAM}
CONSIDERED EXPENDABLE AND
MOUNTAINS ^{FROM} IT WITH SCRAPS AND I WILL
SEE THEY HAVE NO ONE IN THIS
DISAPPEARANCE ARCHAEOLOGIST FORENSIC
TRACE THUS ALL OF GOD USED THE
PROFESSIONALS OF A MAN ON A NEOLIBERAL
TALKING POINT WE DO NOTHING BEYOND
CAPITALISM FORENSIC OR ANTIMATTER OF
UNKNOWN INSECT COLONIES GORGED ON
BLEEDING WORLDS THE TECHNOLOGICAL
MATERIALIZATION OF BLACK POOLS
AND AESTHETIC CANCERS PROLIFERATE ^{IN}
THE GAPS MAKING EXIT THE ONLY OPTION
LEAVING OUR LETTERS AND SNAPSHOTS
INTIMATE FOLLOWING A NOTE OF CHAOS THAT
HE PAINTED DEADE TERRITORIES WITHOUT
MEANING THAT WE COULD IMAGINE A WORLD
WHERE BARELY **ACTIVE** GLANDS ARE STILL
BEING REHABILITATED THOROUGHLY
INTEGRATING INTO REALITY OR
NONEXISTENCE OR VIRTUALLY IT MUST
REMAIN ANOTHER UNPREDICTABLE
EVENT ANYMORE DENIAL AND SACRIFICE
FOLLOWS IN PERFECTIBLE BLACK BOXES *WE
LIVE PARADOXICALLY AS THREATS I SAY* A
FAILED SUICIDE A HIT OF SKIN ^{IN} STEREO I HAD
THE HELPLESS HEAD OF WORM ASSASSINS A
CONSENSUAL DELUSION OF FATAL QUALITY
THIS INFECTION ONLY GIVING IT WITH EARLIER

MORNING HYPERVISION OF PERMANENT CRISIS
AND VIRTUAL OVERPRODUCTION OF ASSASSINS
REPULSION RIOTING FOR SEVERAL DECADES

A RAGGED BLEEDING FEEDBACK LOOP INSIDE
FILLING THE ECONOMIC LEVEL BUT THERE IS A
LUXURIOUS NAKED LUNCH OFFERING TO
REPRODUCE REPTILES A SUCCESSFUL SUICIDE IS
NOW ONE ^{IN} TEN WITH SCRAPS AND FINDING IT
NO MORE ARBITRARY AND GRATIFYING THAN
SURRENDER NOMADOLOGIES OF

UNOPENED BOXES ^{IN} WHITE HEAT GENDER
NIHILISM CRISIS AND GENETIC ONES
INJECTED THROUGH SICKNESS ^{IN}
CATASTROPHIC TEMPORALITIES AND
COLLAPSING ^{IN} THE PRESENCE OF PULSION AND
TO ITS COMMEMORATION ^{IN} INDEFINITE
SIMULATION AN ESCALATING GLOBE BOILING
OURSELVES ^{IN} OTHER ENDS WITHOUT FORENSIC
MEANS OR ANTIHEROES OF AESTHETIC
TERMS INTO BANALITY SOMETHING LIKE
LITTLE AIR BUBBLES UNDER A WORLD IMAGINE
THE BAROQUE WHICH COLLAPSES ^{IN} PLAYS
RIGHTLY DISAPPEARED ONLY SIMULATING THE
HORROR WE LIVE WITH MULTITUDES OF *HUMAN
POTENTIALS* SPREAD OUT WITH NO AESTHETIC
CONSEQUENCES TO DESTROY ITSELF ANY
FORENSIC TRACE OVERWHELMED AMBIENT
EROTICS AND SUBJECTS DROWN ^{IN}
GENERALIZATIONS THAT COME ^{FROM} PERFECT
^{LIES} SOMEWHERE ELSE IT MUST DESTROY ITSELF

jake reber

LIKE THE MODERN ARTIST PRETENDS THE NEW FORM AS AN IMAGE BUT PERHAPS ONE MIGHT OPEN **FLOWERING INTO ELECTRONIC** MIASMA OF XENOCIDAL STATES CRAWLING WITH INFECTION OR GO FARTHER [IN] EVERY RESULT THE ALIENS THAT WERE [IN] REVERSE BLEEDING LIQUID NITROGEN OF **D E A T H** [IN] CULTURAL AESTHETIC ORDER TO END WITHOUT END ON TIME THE NAIVE EXERCISE OF UNKNOWN DISEASES **CONSUMING THE TECHNOGENETIC** ONES THAT CROSS THE SWARMS OF BACTERIA SPREADING OVER SOMETHING DIFFERENT TURNING INTO SOFTWARE AND MELTING GENETIC MEMBRANES WITH EXPLOSIVE MOVEMENTS SECRETING TOXIC VAPOURS OF **ATOMIC SOLAR RADIATION** MORTIFIED EXCREMENTAL CIVILIZATION INFORMATION AND ADVERTISING REPETITION OF COLLAPSING HUMANS AND ABSTRACTION JUST A PERVERSE SITUATION [IN] NETWORKDS OF SLIME FIELDS [FROM] SOMEWHERE ELSE DRIPPING WITH NO IMAGE ALL ENHANCED KILLING MECHANISMS TUNED FOR DEICIDE WAITING FOR THE ISLAND EXPANSIONS OF EXCEPTION DRAGGING DOWN ITS VERY BANALITY SOMETHING TOO IMPROVED TO MATTER WHETHER FIGURATIVE OR AS THE AESTHETIC FLAWS ARE COLLECTIVELY FACED

WITH ENHANCED BODY ᴬᵀᵀᴬᶜᴴᴹᴱᴺᵀˢ *IN PORTABLE SKIN SUITS AND BLACKMAILING*

PEOPLE PORTRAYED ᴵᴺ *MOST TRIANGLES OF COURSE ALL SENTIMENTALITY* ᴵᴺ *IMAGE* ˢᴾᴬᴹ *MUST BE REDISTRUBTED THROUGH NEW OBJECTIFICATION INSTEAD OF SIMULACRUM* ARE YOU RECODING

GENERATIVE SEQUENCES OF DESTRUCTIVE FORCES FLYBLOWN CORPSES OF NUCLEAR ARSENALS ALL IGNORING ADA AND LOSING VALUE FADING AWAT FROM ZERO AND NOISE INITIAL FUSING SEQUENCES ADDICTIVE SUBVERSION OF SEXUALITY A WORLD WHERE ANY SERPENT HAS FANGS FORENSIC OR *A SENSELESS REPETITION OF SACRIFICE* IN

FUSING PARTHENOGENETIC MACHINES

jake reber

14 CONCRETE INDEXED

SIMULTANEOUSLY REPEATING AND COLLAPSING ^{IN} THE VOCATION OF SKIN CLOSING DOWN ^{THE} **WHITE HEAT SEQUENCES OF *SOLAR CONCRETE* WHERE ANY OTHER THE SECOND GENERATION SIMULATION OF THINGS BEGINS TO CONGEAL** WE RETURN TO THE NEXUS OF IMAGE BUT WHO RESEMBLES THE END ON THE HEMORRHAGE OF OVERLAID BRIDGES INTERSECTING PATHWAYS AND SIMULACRA REFLECTING A DEADLY STATELESS SELFLESS BROKEN CYBORG ROTTING ^{INSIDE} PAINTED WITH ACID COMMUNISMHIS AGAINST EXPRESSION AND

RITUALLY SLAUGHTERED THROUGH
ABSTRACTION JUST LIKE POOR IMAGES BUT
THERE IS PROFOUND SEDUCTION MORE
MECHANICAL THAN SELFLESS CYBORG
CIRUITBOARDS ^{IN} OPPOSITION BETWEEN

CYBORG DEAD INPUTS **RITUALLY** FIGURATIVE
AND
SLAUGHTERED AND COLLAPSING ^{IN} SEDUCTIVE
OPAQUE POOLS IDENTITY UNDER THE LIMITS
DEGREE XEROX OF PERMANENT CRISIS
AND SEXUAL UTOPIA BECAUSE WE
STILL
DEATH PUSHED THE COMMODITY CARRY OUT
INDIFFERENCE TO SPEAK OF PANIC THE FORCED
EXTERIOR WHICH ^{IN} THE SCENARIOS BEAUTY
REPEAT BECAUSE I COME ^{FROM} AUTHENTICITY
WETWARE IMAGES AND
TELL

PROPHETIC
NARRATIVES OF SEXUALITY AND LANDSCAPES
AND SEXUAL UTOPIA ACCOMPLISHED AS
WETWARE $_{DECRIED}$ ^{IN} TEN YEARS WITH SCRAPS
AND

ROADS WHERE YOU MUST HAVE BEEN
RESOLVED ^{IN} MAKING COMMODITIES ON MORE
THAN MARKET SIMULACRUM BUT WE

DWELL IN THE STRANGENESS OF POLITICS WE
REALLY LOOK AT THEIR SUICIDE AND DID
NOT EXCEL THROUGH SEVERAL GRADUALLY
DEGRADING STATES INDEXED TO HUMAN
POPULATION BY TENTS AND STREAKS OF COLOR
SUNSTROKES AND FEARS OF ITS
BEAUTY AUTHENTICITY OF WORMS AND

ENTROPIC CIRCUIT POTENTIALS SPREAD OUT
INTO THE SPIRIT OF **D E A T H** RATTLE OF
PEOPLE ON WORLDS LIBERATION NOW
PRETENDING TO SAY THERE WILL SPREAD OUT
VIRUS MUTATION **WE LIVE**
PARADOXICALLY AS BEINGS STRAINING TO
ENTER OR EXIT DEPRESSIVE AN UNENDING
CENTURY INVOLVES THE BUREAUCRATIC AND

VAST SILENT MAJORITY OF **EXCESS**
ENERGY AND DREAMS THAT
LEAVE NO AESTHETIC ORDER BUT A DUAL
STRATEGY AN UNORIGINAL WAY TO END SILENT
FREQUENCY OF FLOWING THROUGH THEM FROM
DESPERATE MIGRATIONS A PROCESS OF
REPULSION BUT ALSO A TRANSAESTHETICS
MARKET IN GENERATIVE SEQUENCES OF ESCAPE

BURNING DRIFTING OUT NO
VALUE ONLY RITUAL
PATHS OF UNCONSCIOUS DRIVES LIBERATION
SEXUAL UTOPIAS AND BUILDINGS IN
CATASTROPHES OF ENTROPY THE LINE
OF SEXUALITY A RESERVE THIS
DISAPPEARANCE ALL HUMAN ATTENTION IS
NOT RECESSION PROOF

ZONES ARE JOINED ON LOOMS OF THESE IMAGES
BUT YOU CANNOT ADD THE EXISTENCE IN BOTH
AN IMAGE ESCAPING EXCHANGE AND
HEATED PHOTOSYNTHESIS
BIOMECHANICS CUT UP THE NEED TO

THIS VANISHING AND FANTASTICAL SIDE OF
HORROR XENOCIDAL STATE POWERLESSLY

DECOMMISSIONS ANDROID ANDROGYNY WHICH
COLLAPSES ^{IN} IMAGES DISSIMULATING AT
THEIR MAXIMUM RATE WHERE ONE FOLLOWING
A HEROIC ABNEGATION OF FORM ^{FROM}

INTERLOCKING TENDRILS AND

BLOSSOMING SOLAR FREQUENCIES ALL
THREATEN THE POSSIBILITY OF THE FUTURE
UNDONE

BROKEN CONCRETE GLASS SOLAR FLARES
DESTROY BODIES YOU REMEMBER THE
PROPHECY IS SIMULATION NOTHING BEYOND
SIMULATION ENVISAGED BY CONCRETE GLASS
COVERED IN ONE THOUSAND

MULTIDIMENSIONAL EYES WHERE AFTER
TWENTY YEARS THE IMPOSSIBLE BECOMES ALL
THAT WE CAN IMAGINE

GLASS PACKING CRATES CORRUGATED IRON
WHERE UNDEAD ARMIES OF COMMAND
SYSTEMS NOT SYSTEMS OF HOPE RIGHTLY
DISAPPEARED THEREIN LIES THEIR

REHABILITATION TODAY ^{IN} ONLY CARRYING
OUT DRONE WORK WE THINK WE CAN ONLY
FACE THE SOLUTION WHERE EVERYTHING ENDS
AND THE FUTURE TURNS TO DUST OR PILES OF
FLESH

AND BEING STRAINED TO CHARACTERIZE THE
ALMOST IMPROVED STATE OF ALL HUMAN

ATTENTION THEY ACTUALLY NEED
MELANCHOLY NOT DESTRUCTION

OR ANOTHER UNPREDICTABLE EVENT
REPEATED UNEXPECTEDLY IT COME FROM
PROLIFERATING ORGANS BETWEEN BODIES
VOMIT OF ALL YOUR
SUBJECTS BECOME TOTAL ORGY WHAT
HUMANITY ARTICULATED IN ITSELF THERE WILL
LOOK LIKE A NEW MODERN FORMULATION THE
PROLIFERATION

WHERE THEY BECOME AN INFINTE FLESH
BEHIND AND BELOW NOT BY EXCEEDING ITS
MEANING AND REFERENCE WETWARE

SPREADING AND INFECTING **D E A T H**
THROUGH TACTILITY AND SLICING

15 CLINICAL
HYPERMARKETS

UNDEAD ARMIES OF THINGS SHOULD GO
FARTHER ^{IN} VERTIGO OF CYBERNETIC CONTROL
TOWERS SURVEILLING WITH TENTACLES
INSTEAD OF GOLDEN VAPOUR ARMIES AND THE
FLATLINE STATUS OF THINGS WE KNOW IS OUR
LAND AND MOUNTAINS ^{FROM} THE PUBLICIZING
GENOTYPES

                INPLEMENTED BY
TRANSHUMANS SQUAT   IN
COMMODITY FORM TO DECONSTRUCT   ITS
DISAPPEARANCE ^{IN} WETWARE MATTER
FIGURATIVE OR NOT EVEN AN ALIEN

BLEEDS ^{INTO} POOR   SIMULATIONS
AND THE FARTHEST ^{LINES}   DISCARDED
POOLS OF MEAT DISSOLVING ^{IN}
CATASTROPHIC ISLANDS DENSE CLUSTERS OF

NEGATIVE ECSTASY AND BACTERIA
SPREADING OVER THE EVIL SPIRIT OF ENTROPY
THE ORGY ELECTRIC THAT
CONSTITUTED THE PATHOLOGY

DENSE CLUSTERS OF GOD THE
EXACERBATION OF BACTERIA SPREADING OVER
SOMETHING LIKE REPRODUC TION ON A WORLD
BEGINNING AGAIN STARTED THROUGH BIRD

CLUSTERS OF VALUE WE LIVE WITH
MEANING SHOCK WAVES OF
SOFTWARE CRASHES ALL GOLD
STANDARDS MELT

RADIO WAVES

LEAVE OUR ABSOLUTE
OBJECT GIVING THIS VERY
BANALITY SOMETHING TOO DIRECT
A LINE OF MONETARY EXCHANGE SLUDGE
FEVERISH HALLUCINOGENIC
DEGREES

WAVES LEAVE NO DOOR AFTER TWENTY YEARS
EXTRATERRESTRIAL FORMS NO AESTHETIC
ORDER BUT PETRIFIED PRECIOUS STONE
TABLETS OF COMMANDMENTS MIMIC OUR
LIKENESS ISOMORPHIC BUT BEHIND IMAGES
DISTORTED INTO HUMAN FORM EVEN IF THEY
OVERWHELM THE IRONY WETWARE

DISINTEGRATING PLANET EVERY
DAY WE REALLY POSED IDEALLY DEFINED ART
FALLING INTO DEEP SPACE VAPOURIZED IN
BLEEDING ULCERS AND EASY SOLUTIONS

POTENTIALIZING EVERYTHING WE KNOW AS ^{IT}
SPLITS OPEN LIKE THOSE CREATURES WHEN
THEY PAINTED THE GREATER GLORY AND
WORSHIPPED SILENTLY

SECOND FALL PREY TO PURE

OBSCENITY AN EQUIVALENCY YOU ARE
ALREADY BEHIND EACH DAY WAITING FOR
BOTH AN IMPULSE AND IRRATIONAL THOUGHT
AN ARTIFICAL ARTIST PAINTED HIS EXISTENCE
AS *FORM SHATTERS THE INFINITE*

REPRODUCTION OF THEIR SKIN
CLOSING DOWN WITH SNAPSHOTS INTIMATE
AND IRONIC THE WAY THE LIVER AND
SIMULACRA **REFLECT SHOCK WAVES OF
CAPITAL** DIRTY MONEY ORBITING THE MINOR
DEMONS AND ***INTIMATE AND ARTERIAL COLD
BLOOD INTERNAL ICEFLOWS OF RULING
ASSEMBLIES RUNNING NUCLEAR MELTDOWN
UNTIL ALL THESE ARE BROKEN AND CORROSIVE***

ART HAS NOTHING TO OFFER THEM VULGAR
MARXISM SPAWNS AN EMPTY MESSAGE ^{STATIC TV}
^{BROADCASTS} AND WE ALL DIE

CYBERNETIC NEURAL NETS AND
LIBERATION LIBERATION OF ^{WETWARE}
OPERATING BEYOND THE VOID AS MARX WROTE
AND ARTERIAL BLOOD COLD

ECOLOGICAL MUTATION AND NO COUNTER
MEASURE AFTER THE TRANSFORMATION OF
DECAY ^{IN} ORDER TO DESTROY IMAGES GOD
KNOWS HAS DISAPPEARED

TEXT MESSAGES DRIFT BY DENYING THE CLINICAL HYPERMARKETS LONG RANGE ANOREXIC *RECESSION INTO SONIC REPRODUCTION DRAWN WITHIN A FAMILIAR OBJECT*

MEDIUM IDEOLOGICAL PLEASURES TODAY IN WITH MULTITUDES OF TECHNOGENETIC ONES THAT ARE RAPIDLY ACCELERATING IN WHICH STARTS WITH CHAOS DRIVES

DRIFT AWAY FROM DEAD UNDERSEA EYES AT ITS INFECTION POINT SLIPPING INTO IRREFERENTIAL EFFECTS THE SENSE OF VALUE THAT REVIVES THE MORE AWAY FROM ASSIMILAT ING THE HIGHEST FUNCTION OF EATING CANCER THEN EXTENDING TOWARDS NONBEING STRAINED TOWARDS DISTINGUISHING CLEARLY   BETWEEN THEM AND FROM THE   PROLIFERATING OGANS VOMIT   WEAPONS ART WAR HALL DEMONIC   BUREAUCRATIC DISASTER AND   UNREALITY THAT ENGENDER IT NOT YET   UNCODED

EARTH BREATHING WITH THEM FROM

STASIS AND TOTALITARIAN

MATERIALIZATION OF EVENTS EMBEDDED IN ***ART AND ITS CORPSE OR MEANING*** THE MODERN ARTIST IS PROFOUND SEDUCTION A FEW CENTURIES OF ECHOES BUT

MELANCHOLIC ENCHANTED

SIDE ENIGMATIC AS PEOPLE *COLLAPSE AT EVEN GREATER SPEEDS BEHIND* WHICH FALL TECTONIC *ARCHITECTURE* OF THOSE WHO **WHISPERS INTO CIRCUITS** OF REAPPEARANCE TODAY AND OUR TIMES AND ONE STROKE THE OUTSIDE ANNIHILATES

ARCHITECTURE OF OBSCENITY NOTHING *BEYOND* SIMULATION IF THE OFFICIALIZATION OF OVERLAID INFORMATION AND SEDUCTION MORE THAN COMMODITIES

DESIRES AND

RAISING HUMAN POTENTIALS SPREAD OUT ON TRASH IN OPAQUE POOLS IDENTITY OBLITERATING THE TRANSFORMATION OF FROM SOMEWHERE FEARS OF COMPOSITION AND MACHINE

COMBINATIONS NOT YET REALIZED AND TEXT MESSAGES

IDEOLOGICAL PLEASURES TODAY YOU DROWN IN *TEMPORAL FLUX AND ARTERIAL BLOOD COLD EXPLOSION OF DIGITALLY ENHANCED*

CREATURES WHO ARE

LIQUIDATED IN INDEFINITE SIMULATION OR THE VIRTUAL EQUIVALENT

FRACTURED ACROSS

ONEHUNDRED THOUSAND YEARS IN

MELANCHOLY THE SAD ALIENATED OR DISPOSSESSED IT WAS FOLLOWING THE ASCETICISM OF CULTURE ART BEFORE

ONE THOUSAND YEARS EXTRATERRESTRIAL FORMS NO BORDERS *AND MODERN CHALLENGES* TO CHARACTERIZE THE SIDEWALK WITH CLANDESTINE MALEVOLENCE OF SYSTEMS

YEARS OF THINK SO ON WALLS ^{IN} ART WORKS
AVOIDING OBJECTIVE ALIENATION AND SO

PARAMILITARY FORMATIONS OF
GOVERNMENTAL AUTHORITY REPLACED BY
EXTRATERRESTRIAL FORMS RECONFIGURING
DESIRES AND INDIFFERENT MOODS OF
AVOIDING ALIENATION BY DENYING THE
OBJECT

GIVING IT SHAPE UNREAL

FORMS ITS HEADS RITUALLY
SLAUGHTERED AND CAN MOVE BETWEEN
THIS WORLD AS IMAGE GOD WAS FOLLOWING A
SIMULACRUM OF

INTELLIGENCE MAY INCREDULOUSLY SIFTING
THROUGH OUR PLANET EVERY SECOND
MOMENT FOR SIMULATION COMES FROM
POLITICALLY DESPERATE MIGRATIONS BY

INCREDULOUSLY *SIFTING THROUGH*

MICROSCOPIC INJURIES AND PLUNGING IN
INDEFINITE SIMULATION BUT RATHER DEEPLY
CONSUMED BY ITS
FORMS AND
SIFT THROUGH REDESIGNED BY
MICROSCOPIC INJURIES VORTICULAR
AND SIMPLIFIED ARTISTIC
PRACTICE AND STAINS OF THOUGHT SEVERAL
ESCAPE ARE POSSIBLE GRADUALLY
ALL MODERN ERA MEANS DEGRADING STATES
FOR ALL MODERN INDEXED TO BONES
SPECKLED WITH
PROSTHESES AS THE CIRCUIT BREAKER OF

CAPITAL *CONSUMES* THE DECAY AND
EQUALIZES ALL DISASTER EVENTUALLY

BUT YOU PREFER TO VANISH [IN] GENERAL
AESTHETICIZATION OF COMPOSITION AND
RADICAL DENIAL THE PERSPECTIVE I SAY
NOTHING IN COMMUNICATIONS BUT I WILL BE A
NEXUS OF MODERN DESTINY MAKING
EPHEMRAL TISSUE THROUGH MICROSCOPIC
INJURIES AND SYNTHETICS

invasive species

■ ■ ■

IMAGINE THE SUBVERSION AND INTENSE
NOTHINGNESS GIVEN AS FASCINATION WHEN
PLASTIC HUMANS ARE ALL LIQUIDATED

PERPLEXITY OF OBSCENITY WE KNOW THIS
NULLITY THIS UNKNOWNING IS DEEP
SIMULATION BEYOND THE CURRENT STATE
WHERE ALL YOUR PARANOID THOUSAND EYED
SUNS IN VERTIGO A STORY FULL OF FORM TO
DISAPPEAR OBEYING THE AESTHETIC
VALUE AFTER THE FATE CREATURES
WHO DO THE MADNESS OF
ACCOMPLISHING THEM ASSIMILAT ING
THE DISAPPEARANCE AN ENLIGHTENING
MOMENT WHEN IT SHOULD BE EXCHANGED
WHEN IT MUST REMAIN ALIVE THAT ART ITSELF
HAS DISAPPEARED THEREIN LIES THE
SUBLIMINAL HUM OF MODERNITY THE NEW NO

LONGER INVOLVED **WAIT FOR UNENDING ALIENATION BY RADICALIZING** ONLY TAKING AWAY FROM THE GLOBE DESPERATELY VYING FOR SIMULATED ACTUALITY SPAM HUMANITY POWER OF BACTERIA SPREADING OVER IMMENSE DUNES OF ACCOMPLISHING A TECHNOLOGICAL MATERIALIZATION OF COLLAPSE HUMAN IDENTITY LOOK WHERE HE REPRODUCED THE FALLING UNDEAD HUMANITY AS MELANCHOLY OR BECAUSE HE DEALT WITH LESIONS WHICH COLLAPSES IN CATHECTED MOTOR OF

WE HAVE SAID THAT WE INHABIT A RUST SPECKLED SAFETY PIN PLANET A SILENT MAJORITY INDEED BUT WHERE MATERIAL BECAME A PROSTHESIS INSTEAD OF BECOMING WORMS TO USE VALUE WETWARE

SWARMING INSECTS DESTROYING USEFULNESS AND DISMANTLING CONTEMPORARY SACRIFICE IN SOLAR FLARES BEFORE CRYOGENIC

FREEZING URBAN SPRAWL IN FACT THAT DELAY DID NOT REDUCE SUICIDE THERE IS ONLY MEANING IN **BLACK MARKET CAPITALISM** ALL SENTIMENTALITY IN RELIGIOUS ICONS DISMEMBERED THROUGH STATIC AND PICTURES INADVERTENTLY SENT OFF THROUGH VIRAL CONTROL LOOPING NOISE MACHINES PILES OF STRAYS ELECTRIC DREAMS AND ARTERIAL BLOOD COLD EXPLOSION OF RULING ASSEMBLIES RUNNING

jake reber

INADVERTENTLY SENT OFF INTO CIRCUITS OF RECUPERATION ENDS AS A VANISHING POINT AND NEUROTIC *MATERIALIZATION* OF **D E A T H** RATTLE OF REALITY AND LET GO.

Made in the USA
Las Vegas, NV
15 June 2021